Ian was on cloud nine as he waltzed Laney all around the dance floor.

Like another scene from a movie. Dancing around the room as if the two of them were the only people there.

Romance.

There it was. That forbidden word. The word his family thought was silly nonsense at best and a destructive force at worst. Yet it was something he'd always dreamed of experiencing. Was that something he could safely pretend at this week, too?

Not safe at all, a fact not to be forgotten. Laney was what was firing him up in the first place, making him think about things like soulmates and joy and passion. There was a list of reasons Laney could never be the woman for him. First of all, she'd made a vow to remain single, so she wasn't even available. Second, he knew that his family expected him to partner with someone from their exclusive and privileged world. Most importantly, most dangerously, was that he could never have a calculated and loveless agreement with her.

No, around her his blood ran hot.

The only possibility with her was impossibility: the real deal.

Dear Reader,

Just as I might ask other authors, readers ask me what my inspiration might be for a particular book. For this one, it was my hero. I had a clear picture of Ian in my mind, how he looked, talked, moved, felt. A man loyal to his family and their livelihood but a romantic at heart, and who gets to live out some of his charming fantasies, like rowing a beautiful woman in a boat on a pond. (Of course, I interrupted the bliss with a surprise for him!) Throughout the story I agonized for him and made sure that, as long as he had Laney by his side, his ever after would be happy.

Another inspiration for this book was pink sand. Yes. Pink. Sand. I've yet to visit a place where the beaches were pink. But looking at some photos of Bermuda, I thought that was one of the most beautiful sights I'd ever seen, and wouldn't it be lovely to let Laney and Ian spend time there? That is, between Boston, where they start, and New York, where their relationship takes a major turn.

So, there we have it. Ian and pink sand, my sparks for this story. Enjoy!

Andrea x

Pretend Honeymoon with the Best Man

—

Andrea Bolter

Recycling programs
for this product may
not exist in your area.

ISBN-13: 978-1-335-73718-2

Pretend Honeymoon with the Best Man

Copyright © 2023 by Andrea Bolter

For questions and comments about the quality of this book,
please contact us at CustomerService@Harlequin.com.

Harlequin Enterprises ULC
22 Adelaide St. West, 41st Floor
Toronto, Ontario M5H 4E3, Canada
www.Harlequin.com

Printed in U.S.A.

Andrea Bolter has always been fascinated by matters of the heart. In fact, she's the one her girlfriends turn to for advice with their love lives. A city mouse, she lives in Los Angeles with her husband and daughter. She loves travel, rock 'n' roll, sitting at cafés and watching romantic comedies she's already seen a hundred times. Say hi at andreabolter.com.

Books by Andrea Bolter

Harlequin Romance

Billion-Dollar Matches collection

Caribbean Nights with the Tycoon

Her Las Vegas Wedding
The Italian's Runaway Princess
The Prince's Cinderella
His Convenient New York Bride
Captivated by Her Parisian Billionaire
Wedding Date with the Billionaire
Adventure with a Secret Prince

Visit the Author Profile page
at Harlequin.com for more titles.

For STAY

**Praise for
Andrea Bolter**

"From that first book I was completely hooked with her stories and this is easily my all-time favorite to date. I thoroughly enjoyed this, [as] it's the perfect little escapism."

—*Goodreads* on *Captivated by Her Parisian Billionaire*

CHAPTER ONE

"THAT FLOWER ARRANGEMENT is blocking Melissa's face a little bit."

"It's fine."

"It's not. Help me move it," urged Laney Sullivan, the maid of honor that best man Ian Luss had just met yesterday.

They were watching the bride and groom prepare for rehearsal dinner photos to be taken next to a mammoth display of orange gladiolas.

"Come on, Ian."

Really not agreeing that they should be the ones to make any adjustment, he hesitated. "Wait for the photographer," he said, reiterating his opinion.

"You're not going to get your nice suit dirty, if that's what you're worried about." That wasn't his concern, although it was a valid one. They weren't in wedding attire, as the big event was tomorrow, but were dressed for the dinner and the photo shoot that had been scheduled. In his bespoke navy suit, he needed to stay preened and tucked into photogenic readiness. However, his true objection to Laney's request was that they were at the Fletcher Club, Boston's most austere and opulent private establishment. The premiere wedding destination in town no doubt had staff assigned for every task under the sun. He and the maid of honor did not need to be touching the flowers.

After a run-through of the ceremony on the twenty-seventh harbor-view floor where Melissa Kraft and Clayton Trescott would marry, they'd adjourned and traveled one floor down to the cocktail lounge, which offered a panoramic vista of downtown. At twilight the sky was a glinting blue, the city beginning to twinkle into evening. An area near the windows had been stanchioned off with velvet ropes for the photo session, where the Custom House Tower, Faneuil Hall and more city landmarks would serve as the backdrop.

Melissa wore a tight dress in emerald-green, the wedding party color, as she hung on Clayton's arm while they chatted with guests. Ian knew Clayton from university days and they'd stayed close over the years.

His friend was clearly head-over-heels smitten with his bride, his sparkling eyes telling the tale. Ian had no wife or girlfriend but couldn't imagine being married to a woman like Melissa, who never walked past a mirror without looking in it. Who shortly after getting engaged to Clayton made a point of telling Ian, as well as posting on social media, the carat count of her diamond engagement ring.

Truthfully, Ian didn't know what type of woman he'd marry, other than one who understood the basic tenet that a Luss such as himself, of Luss Global Holdings, considered marriage as a strategic merger, just as his family's acquisitions of land were. Marriage was a big thing to the Lusses, although not in the way most people would think of it. Position and thorough breeding were everything. Love and passion were not factors. At thirty, he was expected to make one of those fortuitous marriages soon.

To the matter at hand, in addition to not moving the flowers Laney was worried about, another way Ian didn't think he should get involved with things would be in mentioning to the maid of honor that her hair was a mess and needed attention. It had probably been carefully styled earlier, and now, for whatever reason, several golden locks had escaped the twisty roll they'd been sculpted into. The errant strands looked less like they were well thought out to frame her face or give a sexy allure and were, instead, more like she was a kid who had been out playing in the yard wearing her fancy clothes after she was told not to. It was actually kind of cute, like she didn't really care about her appearance. Although it wouldn't do, and hopefully, a female member of the wedding party would take her aside and smooth everything back into place.

A couple of guests milling around took out their phones and began snapping candid shots of the bride and groom, the prephoto photos. Next, would some other group take photos of the group taking photos of the prephotos for the prewedding?

He knew that he'd be going through some wedding traditions himself before long. In fact, his grandfather Hugo had begun speaking with some of his old cronies, the wealthiest men in New England, to check on the marital status of their granddaughters. That's how the Luss family did things, nothing left to chance after a couple of slipups had almost brought their fortunes to the ground.

He glanced over to Clayton and his big smile, admiring his happiness. Ian's own wedding surely wouldn't be the best day of his life like it might be for an enchanted groom. That was all right, he told himself. Everyone had their roles in life.

"Just help me for a minute."

Ian heard the words enter his ears while he stared at Clayton, wondering what this moment was like for him. Pure, unadulterated joy and certainty about his life ahead of him? What did expressions of love feel like, Ian wondered, as the groom kissed his bride's cheek? What really was romance? He'd seen examples of it, watched other couples in action, but he didn't know what it did to someone on the inside?

Ian's grandfather, and all the way back to his grandfather's grandfather, were probably right that emotional distractions could be costly, and an amicable business-type partnership was best. Love, but without the intensity of being *in love*. After all, it took steely determination to amass an empire such as theirs. Still, as Ian watched Clayton's hand slide around Melissa's waist, he mused on the trade-off, on what he might miss out on. What he'd always read about in books and seen in movies. Courtship! Heart song! Passion!

"Ian, Earth is calling. Just help me out for a minute," Laney repeated, snapping him out of his trance.

The maid of honor was still adamant that the flowers needed some sort of tweak, so she wrapped her fingers around his forearm and gave him a little tug toward the staging area. A strange shock ran through him at her touch, like an electrical current. It was a wholly unfamiliar sensation, and he eyed her disapprovingly for causing it.

She enlisted him to help her rotate the tall glass cylinder of flowers so that the offending bloom was no longer obscuring her cousin Melissa's face.

"Edge it that way," she gestured.

As they did so, the official photographer arrived with cameras around her neck. All of the amateur cell phone snappers respectfully took a step backward.

"Satisfied?" he asked Laney, regarding the flowers, although the difference was minuscule. The bride's larger-than-life orange-lipped grin faded the colors of everything else around them. Yet again, he watched the radiance that took over Clayton's face at his bride's every move. A lurch gripped Ian's stomach. Still, he wondered what love might feel like, literally how it might inhabit the cells of someone's body. How it could influence thought. Maybe even have an involuntary effect on breathing. All things he had never experienced and probably never would. Well, there was that one talk he had with his late grandmother Rosalie, but that was years ago. His friend's wedding was prompting a lot of questions Ian had never asked before.

"It seemed easier to do it than wait around," Laney said beside him.

"Fine. Whatever," Ian said. The photographer brought her meters to Melissa's face and then to Clayton's. "Are you due in makeup before the shoot?"

Whereas the bride and the bridesmaids who were filing into the room were wearing the world's current supply of makeup, they hadn't seemed to have left any for Laney, because she didn't appear to have a drop of it on. Her skin was pale and untouched, and her lips their given shade of dusty pink. Truth be told, she was absolutely lovely, natural and real, even with that messy hair. Yet he was curious if she'd forgotten that one of her duties as maid of honor was to tolerate what was sure to be a barrage of photos in various settings. She was on the shorter side and was dressed for tonight's festivities in a slinky silver dress that showed off major curves he attempted not to pay too much attention to.

"No, I don't wear makeup," Laney answered defiantly, as if she'd been accused of something. "I've tried it, and it's so itchy it makes my skin crawl."

She looked down to her fingernails and rubbed them as if she was making sure they were clean. She didn't have nail polish on either, another convention he was used to seeing on women wearing dressy clothes. Clayton had told him that Laney was moving back to Boston after a failed attempt at running a café in Pittsfield, in the scenic Berkshires region of Western Massachusetts. She surely had the look of someone who spent more time doing something with her hands than she did with them in a manicurist's shop. Clayton had also mentioned something about an ex.

In any case, based on her sharp response he might have insulted her in asking about the lack of makeup. "Forgive me," he said, bringing his palm flat to his chest, "it's just that... I think if you check yourself in the mirror, you'll find that your hair is…a little out of sorts."

She looked him straight in the eyes as her cheeks puffed out as round as they could go, and she exhaled in a slow, steady stream until they deflated. "Thanks for the tip," she said, then pivoted and walked away.

"I was only trying to be helpful," he called after her. "We're best man and maid of honor. Isn't it our job to try to make everything flawless?"

Argh! Saying that she was anything other than flawless was another wrong statement. He was strangely flustered around her, whereas generally, he was in steely control. Not that his words had any effect because Laney and her curves continued sashaying away from him, out of the bar area completely and blasting through the double doors that led to the wedding party's dressing rooms. His eyes stayed on her until a staff member wheeling a cart obstructed his view.

"Okay, fine." Laney surrendered to the makeup artist's third plea to allow a little lip gloss for the photos. She had not been the first choice for maid of honor, and it showed. As the bride's cousin, she was to be a bridesmaid until Melissa's best friend pulled out at the last minute because of a difficult pregnancy. Laney and Melissa could hardly be more unalike and didn't see a lot of each other as children. Laney grew up with a single mom on the wrong side of Boston, whereas Melissa hailed from the wealthy suburb of Wellesley. Laney's mother was never close with her brother, the father of the bride.

"Thank you for filling in," Melissa said as Laney allowed the makeup artist to glob the goop onto her lips.

Laney figured she'd only need to leave it on for the shoot, then they'd go right to dinner, and it would be perfectly legitimate for her to wipe it off. Likewise tomorrow, glop for the ceremony and more photos, slime wiped off for cocktails and hors d'oeuvres. She could manage this.

"You're welcome," said Laney.

The makeup artist finally moved on, and the two returned from the dressing room to the cocktail lounge.

"You were saying on the phone that you've had a hard time of it lately?" the bride asked.

"Yeah, it turned out I was unlucky in both love and business."

This modern fairy-tale wedding of lipstick and party salons high in the sky was what Laney thought she was heading toward when she met Enrique Sanz. He'd come into the Cambridge café near Harvard University where she'd been working and changed her life. Handsome and cultured, he was in Boston after just finishing a master's degree in business. She thought they were in love. He even consented to buying the café in Pittsfield that they ran together. Although he was always reminding her that she was "not the type he could have on his arm forever." Apparently, owning a café was okay for a short time, but it wasn't a lofty enough goal for a man whose family supplied half of Spain with lumber.

"I hope things get better for you," Melissa muttered sympathetically. "Clayton says I could sell my shop, but I'm going to keep it, at least for now."

"Right."

In addition to being a glamazonian piece of eye candy and marrying a high-ranking bank executive, Melissa had a handbag shop in Beacon Hill that attracted the Boston elite. "Of course, we're hoping to get preggers as soon as possible!"

"I wish you the best."

"Hey, you know, there are some really great single men coming this weekend. Don't people say weddings are a great place to meet?"

Sure, as if any man in Melissa's social circle would be interested in her. A wave of irritation swept over Laney as she recalled her own misfortune. The café attempt was a disaster and Enrique broke her heart. Having wedding duties just as she'd returned to town wasn't ideal. However, it was time to put all of that aside and get through this weekend. Then she could start over. That first task might be easier without Ian Luss, the best man, who was now striding toward her. She'd only met him enough to say hello yesterday, but an hour or so ago, when she asked him for help moving the flowers, he seemed lost in space, and she could hardly get his attention.

Then he'd rubbed her the wrong way with telling her that she needed to fix her hair, just like some criticism Enrique might have had. As he approached, he looked straight to her lips, which were now no doubt so shiny he could see himself in their reflection. He was probably gloating about having asked her if she was due in the makeup chair and her defensively proclaiming that she didn't paint her face. Although he might be annoying, she had to admit that he was good-looking, with his big brown eyes and black hair that almost reached his shoulders. He stood tall in his finely tailored suit that fit slim along his broad shoulders and long legs. Not that she found him *attractive* attractive. She was just admiring him as one does a piece of art, for example. Attraction to men could only lead to more trouble. She needed a major life do-over and that would start with steering clear of the male species.

"All right, wedding party, let's gather," the photographer called out. "We'll start with the bride and groom, best man and maid of honor."

"That's us," Melissa bubbled as she left Laney's side to take Clayton's hand.

Ian gestured for Laney to go ahead of him toward the photo spot, which was now set with reflectors to produce the best possible lighting. The photographer had some fun poses, such as one where Clayton held out a single orange rose to Melissa as they stood above a seated maid of honor and best man, Ian gifting Laney a rose as well. Laney's heart thumped a beat at Ian's eyes locking onto hers during the motion, making it an unexpected exchange between them. The wedding party was then brought into the shots, followed by various configurations of family holding flowers of their own.

Afterward, the staging area was quickly dismantled, and waiters dressed in black with gold aprons passed Bellinis from silver trays. Laney made sure to grab a napkin with hers, as her lip goo time was officially over, and she happily wiped it off. Ian, talking to a couple of the groomsmen just a few feet away, caught the move, and the tip of his mouth curled up. She really wasn't sure whether he was cute or aggravating, although it really didn't matter, because she was off men. Plus, she'd never see him again after this wedding. Or until Melissa and Clayton's first baby had a birthday party, or something like that.

Appetizer stations were set out. At the mozzarella sampling bar, Laney was trying a burrata with roasted pistachio when Ian came up beside her. "Are you giving a speech?"

She finished chewing before answering, "I don't know if I'd call it a speech, but they asked me to say a few words tonight and leave the traditional speech to you tomorrow."

He grabbed his throat like he was being choked. "The pressure. The pressure."

"Just say something romantic. That's what brides like," Laney said.

He took in her words as if he'd never heard anything like them before.

He helped himself to a piece of the *fior di latte* cheese on a square of focaccia. "So, what, you don't want to paint your nails and gussy up, but you still want the princess tiara and the happily-ever-after thing? You'll make it tough for a guy to figure out, or are you already spoken for?"

"No one is speaking for me." She grabbed a hunk of that milky *fior* with her fingers and popped it in her mouth.

Ian reached over and flicked a speck of cheese from the front of her dress where it had landed.

She rolled her eyes. "Again? First it was my hair. Then my lack of makeup. Now you're cleaning food off me?"

"You're welcome."

"I'm sure a crumb has never dared touch a piece of your fine woolens, but could you just keep your business to yourself, and I'll do the same with mine?"

"I was only trying to help."

"Don't."

He lifted his palms up in surrender and walked away.

Laney fisted her hands in frustration. She knew he only meant well, but the criticism was hard for her to take. She'd had enough to last a lifetime. Of course, Ian and his comments didn't mean anything to her. He didn't have the ability to wound her as Enrique had with his constant disapproval. Whom she should have known from the beginning wasn't a gentleman, but she was fooled. He'd whispered things into her ear that made her think they were truly together. That he'd take her to live in Madrid with him. It was all so exciting. Until he started picking on her. Where she went, how she looked, what she wore. How drab it was that all she wanted was her own café. In retrospect, she didn't know what she saw in him, except that his European glamour was nothing like the small-minded sons born of the rough streets in Dorchester.

When it was speech time, Laney stood holding a mic in front of the guests seated for the rehearsal dinner. "I know people like to share a famous quote about marriage," she said, continuing her toast. A plate clinked at one table, then another as the waitstaff delivered the salads. Voices here and there were in conversation. She lifted her Bellini. "To Melissa and Clayton. Writer H. L. Mencken said, 'Love is the triumph of imagination over intelligence.'"

What she'd meant as a funny bit of cynicism flopped royally. The room fell silent. The bride's big tangerine smile drooped like a sad clown. Laney looked to Ian at her table. He winced at her failure.

This is going to be a long weekend, Ian thought to himself as he finished the pasta flight that had been set in front of him and each guest at the rehearsal dinner. A wooden board with four carved out grooves had contained corn spaghetti carbonara, pesto potato gnocchi, rigatoni with Bolognese and fusilli with raw tomatoes and basil. He'd made short work of the presentation, as he was hungry, and concentration on his food meant less time blathering about nothing with the groomsman and his wife who sat to his right. They were the only ones to talk to because to his left, Clayton was continuously occupied with well-wishers who approached in an endless parade.

The groomsman and his wife beside Ian were from Albany, New York. She pulled out her phone to show Ian their three children, who hadn't come along to the wedding because they were at summer camp. The woman elaborated excitedly on every activity the kids would be involved in while there, from learning computer coding to performing in musical theater. Ian feigned interest.

Politely excusing himself from the table, he wandered from the dining salon back into the cocktail lounge. It wasn't that kids and summer camp were of no matter. After all, Ian planned on having his own offspring and hoped he'd take pride in their accomplishments. It was only that with the Luss methods for maintaining their fortune, which had already been mapped out for the next century, marriage and family were, first and foremost, matters of practicality and logic. Indeed, that's how his parents treated him and his sister, as coworkers, partners and friends. With regard but without warmth. So he wasn't sure how much exuberance there would be over cell phone photos of science experiments.

Ian never saw his parents engage in the gestures of romance that he noticed with other people and in the arts. He worried that having the sense there was a larger emotional life out there, one he couldn't do without, would prevent him from being able to fit into the box his family was saving for him. He strode to the bar and asked the bartender for a maple whiskey rocks. He took a tight sip and glanced around the mostly empty lounge, as the majority of rehearsal dinner guests were in the main room about to enjoy dessert.

"Was that the worst quote in the world?" Laney headed toward him, her satiny dress giving a little swish with every step. Once again, Ian tried not to get caught eyeing her from top to bottom. She surely filled that dress out nicely with her ample bosom and hips. He looked to her pretty face. "I thought it was going to get a laugh, but I think I bombed."

"You did." He had to chuckle. He didn't want to offend her once more, something he seemed to have a knack for, but he wasn't going to lie. Fortunately, she snickered a little bit herself. "Can I get you a drink?"

"What are you having?"

"Maple whiskey on the rocks."

"I'll have the same."

Ian gestured to the bartender.

"Thanks."

Drink delivered, they both gazed out at the skyline.

"Are you from Boston?"

"Dorchester, born and raised."

"Dorchester?"

"Don't sound so shocked. Melissa and I are related, but we didn't have the same kind of childhood."

"What kind of childhood was that?" So, Laney was a scrapper. Who had survived living in one of the most crime-infested parts of Boston, and it didn't seem to have swallowed her up.

"It was just me and my mom pooling our resources. Not these kinds of resources," she gestured around the posh Fletcher Club.

"Is your mom here?"

"No, she's living in Arizona now. She recently had an operation and couldn't make the journey."

"What about your dad?"

Laney took a sip of her drink. "I never knew him. They weren't really together. He took off once she got pregnant."

Ian gulped at that lack of duty. That was why he'd never do anything to defy his family and would fit whatever mold he had to. The Lusses were unflinchingly loyal. For better or for worse, they took care of each other, ran as a pack. Didn't impregnate women they weren't married to. "Clayton told me you'd left Boston for a while."

"I was in the Berkshires for two years. I only returned this week. I'm still adjusting back to city life."

"Where were you?"

"Pittsfield."

"What were you doing there?"

"Operating a café."

"Hmm." He sipped his drink. "How specific."

"Specific? You mean how small-time and limited."

Uh-oh. Had he replied wrong again? He'd only been trying to make chitchat. As people did when they were getting to know each other. "That's not what I meant."

"What did you mean, then?" She cast her eyes down to her drink and swirled the amber liquid in the glass.

"You were running a café. I'm sure the duties were very clear." He shrugged. "Whereas I have no idea what I actually do all day."

Her eyes shot up to meet his. "How do you figure that?"

"I work with my family. We consider purchases."

"Of what?"

"Land."

"That you buy and build on?"

"No. We buy it and hold it. Sometimes we sell it."

"Land?"

"Yes. Mountain ranges and private deserts, things like that."

"How many 'things like that' does your family own?"

"About three hundred worldwide."

"Hmm. That sounds like you're doing *a lot* of things in a day. What's your part?"

"I consult with appraisers."

"Weren't you named in some list of the city's most eligible bachelors?"

"Embarrassing."

"Mountain ranges," she repeated.

He took another pull on his whiskey. One of the city's eligible bachelors implied that he was some kind of prey. To be snatched up. As much as he nodded his head in acquiesce when his grandfather told him it was time to let him choose a bride for him, in reality, Ian didn't want him to. Sure, he might hit it off with one of the highbrow women chosen for her family's name and history. It was possible that would be the woman he was destined to be with. Although he doubted it.

He knew that marriage could be more than what his family outlined. That with the right person, there could be the state of being in love. And that could be what made life truly worthwhile. A union built when two minds, two hearts and two souls melded together and moved through the world as one. Worse still, he sometimes thought that without that, he might never be completely fulfilled and would die empty. He even had the notion that the someone he was meant to be with really was actually out there for him.

Nonsense. He tried to admonish himself. Everyone had their lot, and his was to continue family traditions that hundreds of Luss employees were counting on. Why fix something that wasn't broken? The Luss family didn't have time for romance. That could be left to others. And the more he let himself dwell on silly fantasies, such as one true love, the harder it was going to be to step into the role expected of him.

"Weddings bring up strange thoughts, don't they?" he asked aloud.

"That's for sure."

"So, why aren't you still running that café?"

"It burned down."

He let out a throat-clearing cough. "It what?"

"An electrical line toppled over and started a fire. By time it was extinguished, the damage was beyond repair."

"Oh, gosh. Was anyone hurt?"

"Thankfully, no. But the insurance wasn't enough to rebuild."

"And it left you out of a job. That's why you're back in Boston."

"Yes, and I was in partnership with someone, and that didn't work out, either."

"Oh, sorry to hear that. What are you planning to do now?"

"It's been a heck of a couple of years. I need to regroup. Restart."

"So, you'll get another job?" He sensed she wasn't telling him everything that was going on with her. That she was hurting. Not that it was any of his concern. "What is it that you really want?"

"I've always wanted my own café, so I had that for a minute. I'll have to start from the bottom again and build back up."

"I'm sure there are lots of stories of the humble barista who rises to the top of the café world."

"The humble barista?"

"I've offended you yet again." He shook his head. "I don't talk to many people outside of work. I'm terrible at small talk." Even if he was to marry solely for the family merger, he was going to have to learn to be pleasant company. Something he wasn't doing very well at with Laney so far.

"Oh, right. You have nothing to talk about with the humble barista."

She started to walk away. Without a thought, his hand reached for her arm. Her skin was so silky it startled him. "Laney, don't go. I'd like to hear about owning a café."

She shook off his hold. "It's late. See you tomorrow."

CHAPTER TWO

"By the powers vested in me by the state of Massachusetts, I now pronounce you husband and wife. You may kiss the bride."

As the officiant concluded the ceremony, Laney stood beside Melissa, holding her bouquet. Like they had rehearsed, Laney handed her own bouquet to the bridesmaid on her right, thereby freeing her hands to hold the bride's formidable array of both pale and vivid orange blooms. As Ian had fulfilled his role of taking care of the wedding rings, the maid of honor and best man executed their duties. They both watched, Ian from his side and Laney from hers, as Clayton took his wife in his arms and kissed her to the cheers of the two hundred in attendance.

The string quartet began the wedding recessional, and Melissa and Clayton turned to glide past the guests down the aisle. It struck

Laney how profound the past twenty minutes had been. Melissa and Clayton had walked to the altar single and returned as a married couple, their lives forever changed and defined by what had happened there. With family and friends to witness the ceremony and help launch them forward. What was before was nevermore. They strode forward as one.

It was what Laney had thought she was going to have. What her mother never had but Laney wanted. And was expecting. What she had begun to plan for in her mind. A future where Enrique was solid and committed to her. Even though she'd been fooling herself, and the signs were there all along. Then, indeed, everything was taken from her. She felt the loss down into her bones.

Laney swallowed hard. This was not the time for self-pity. It was time to move her feet toward the head of the aisle, where she met up with the best man. She hoped they could get through the evening without grating on each other's nerves like they had yesterday. She liked how he looked born to wear his well-tailored tux, even with hair a little longer than was conventional. At last night's rehearsal and dinner, he didn't seem to have a date with him. So she assumed he was alone tonight as well. Did he have a girlfriend, though? Or a boyfriend? Someone stashed away in another city who didn't come to the wedding with him for whatever reason? She wasn't sure, but instinct told her no.

Linking her arm into his, her hand settled on the warmth of his sturdy muscle. He was so…formidable. Substantial. The kind of man a person could wade through the waters with. Her eyes blinked a couple of times as they took their first steps together while she tried not to feel defeated. Things had not gone her way.

"Ceremony went well," Ian whispered into her ear, which prickled from the sensation of his breath. "What did you think of the poem Clayton recited?"

"It rhymed. Need I say more?" She bit her lip to squelch a laugh as the photographer snapped continuously during their march. "The flower girl was adorable."

"She was. Especially when she started picking up all the petals after she'd scattered them."

"A hard worker."

Like her. Laney would make it through this wedding weekend, get a job, and move off her friend Shanice's couch. It wasn't Madrid, where she'd concocted all sorts of scenarios about some perfect life she was going to have there. Boston wasn't the worst place to begin again. Although, the truth was that she was tired. She'd barely caught her breath dealing with the café burning down, then Enrique leaving her a week later. She wished she could get a break. Just for a little while. To rest, relax and plan. Although nothing like that was in her current budget, which was about zero, save for her old roommate Shanice's generosity.

At the end of the aisle, Laney let go of her link to the crook of Ian's arm. And missed the feel of it instantly. *Huh.*

"Best man and maid of honor, please hurry to the mezzanine for first toasts," an attendant called to them.

"Let's go." She gave him a tug and maneuvered them quickly through the crowded area where the guests were assembling. The wedding manager waved them into a side entrance, where they climbed a half flight of stairs onto a raised glass platform that jutted out above the cocktail lounge like a stage in the sky so that all the guests could see them. This was where Melissa and Clayton would make their first appearance.

"Now?" Ian asked, verifying with the manager who handed him a microphone. Melissa had wanted the best man's speech to be before dinner. Laney didn't really have anything to do, but she stood beside him with two flutes of champagne, urging him to take one with his free hand.

He hit all the proper notes. Thanking the guests who came from near and far. Saying how lovely and sweet Melissa was. Congratulating his old friend Clayton on finding his mate. Wishing them a long and happy life together. Whereas Laney had bombed last night with her quote that fell flat, Ian's toast was tasteful and reserved and, well, kind of dull. She'd wished he'd gone out on more of a limb. He ended with a quote by Mignon McLaughlin: "A successful marriage requires falling in love many times, always with the same person."

Laney swallowed hard at that. That was a much more romantic closer than she was expecting from him. Falling in love over and over again. Yes, that did indeed sound like a real marriage. Something Enrique wasn't capable of, or not with her anyway.

Then it was time for the *big wow*. The overheads in the room dimmed so that the fairy lights strung everywhere created a magical glow. Laney and Ian stepped down from the elevated platform, her wobbly on her high heels and grabbing his reliable arm for balance. A spotlight was poised, waiting for the stars of the evening. A voice boomed, "Without further ado, I introduce to you for the first time as husband and wife, Mr. and Mrs. Clayton Trescott."

Melissa and Clayton appeared from within the darkened area and stepped onto the platform and into the spotlight to cheers and applause. Melissa had changed into a mermaid-style gown that glistened like a mirror ball, and her face looked like it was going to crack open from smiling so wide.

Laney and Ian watched from the sideline. She tugged the side of her emerald-green maid of honor gown made of a silk shantung, which was actually scratchy and uncomfortable. They still had a long evening ahead of them.

Laney coached herself again. *Just make it through the weekend.*

The band's horn section jammed as the wedding party bounded through the doors into the reception hall in a gaggle just as the photographer had instructed them to. Then, like a blooming flower, the petals that made up the groomsmen and the bridesmaids opened away from the center. Next, the maid of honor and best man stepped away to reveal the bride and groom who, were met by guests clanging knives against water glasses. In response, they kissed. Melissa had changed into another wedding gown, a custom Ian didn't quite understand yet had witnessed at a few of the upscale weddings he'd been to lately.

He supposed it was simply that women loved to dress up, so why have one wedding dress when you could have six? Yes, six, as the bride at a wedding he'd been to a few months ago had worn. He hoped their marriage was going to last long enough to pay the bill on that wardrobe. Melissa's second dress was a tight-fitting number with a weird extra bottom part that swished like a fish's fin.

Once he and Laney circled the happy couple with the choreography that seemed to him like a square dance's do-si-do and he reunited with Laney, he asked her, "What is a dress that style called?"

They smiled for the photographer, now having mastered bringing their cheeks close to each other for the cute close-up. Ian was determined not to give heed to the delightful feeling of Laney's face near his or the empty sensation every time she pulled it away.

"Mermaid," she answered.

Aha! He was right in his marine reference. "Do you like it?"

"No. The way it comes in tight over her… behind…and then flares out the size of a lace tablecloth."

A waiter presented a tray of purplish cocktails in stemmed tulip glasses. "This is the bride and groom's signature cocktail, the Mel-Clay. Lemon vodka, blueberry cordial and ginger ale."

They each took a purple potion from the waiter's tray. Bespoke cocktails were another part of the careful attention that went into grand weddings these days. Because his friends were around thirty like him, marrying age, Ian had attended a lot of weddings lately. If the wife he'd take someday wanted to look like a strange creature from the sea, what would he care?

"Have you ever been married?" Laney asked.

"Heavens, no," said Ian. "If I had, I'd still be. One and done. You?"

"Never. Like I was telling you, I co-owned

that café with Mr. Almost. When it burned down, so did we."

"Why? The disappointment?"

"Something like that. He blamed me for the fire."

"How so?"

"You name it. Accusing me of not having it inspected thoroughly enough before he bought it. That I didn't have the professional know-how or education to run the operation. That I wasn't on top of the upkeep. In reality, he was ready to break up with me, so he used it as an excuse."

"What a jerk."

Between that and a father that skipped out, she hadn't had much of an example of what a decent man was.

"Do you picture having a big wedding?" Laney asked, moving on from the subject.

"I suppose. My family will want it to be as much a PR event as anything else. It's time for my grandfather to retire, but not until he sees me settled and ready to breed the next in succession for Luss Global Holdings."

"Sounds dreamy." She smirked.

"Anything but. That's kind of the point. The Luss family doesn't spend time or re-sources on emotions." Why did that sound so awful coming out of his mouth? It was true, but it was so cold-blooded. He'd had limited dealings with women thus far, his imagination far more active than he was. The young women who he'd dated during his Oxford years made it their business to find out about his family's wealth and tried to snare him. Their efforts were so insincere they fell into their own traps, making sure he was wary and distrustful of them. His grandfather's plan was at least safer, two families going into partnership for mutual benefit with both parties vetted.

So far, even dating casually, he'd never gotten close to a woman, so he hadn't had to worry about feelings being ignited. He couldn't take any chances at not keeping love at bay and then ruining everything generations of his family had worked so hard for. His great-great-uncle Phillip had almost destroyed the company in its formative years because of a woman. And when Ian was a child, his father's brother Harley had lost them tens of millions of dollars by acting on impulse. Ian's grandfather would see to it that nothing like that ever happened again.

"Did you just say your family doesn't waste resources on emotions?"

"Right. Marriages are trade alliances."

The music quieted and the band leader took the mic. "Ladies and gentlemen, let's welcome the bride and groom for their first dance."

As Ian watched the mermaid and her fisherman take to the center of the dance floor, he felt that little lurch in his stomach as he had earlier. Because it wasn't as cut and dry as he'd just explained to Laney. In his secret heart of hearts, he'd always wanted to experience a little bit of emotional love, just to know what it felt like. To let himself be seduced into a whirlwind romance with a woman, to know that. Even once. Sure, there'd be a risk that it could be like getting lost and not being able to find the way home. Yet, he was a level-headed grown man. He could see his way back from the journey. He was not going to fall into any snares and let his grandfather or the Luss Global employees down. Of course, he had no idea how he'd ever go about something like that. Women had their own ideas and would have no interest in playing his game. Therefore, he smiled wistfully at the man and the fish, and that was that.

"What, you're an anti-romantic?"

He looked around the reception hall and

wondered, if maybe for the first time, what conceptions each and every person here had about love. Old and young, rich and poor, single, married, widowed or divorced. "Anti-romantic? I guess you could say that."

That was his official position and he was sticking to it, even if it wasn't what he really harbored inside. And Laney's sable eyes, the sparkling lights, the passionate purple cocktail and the bride's fish fin of a dress were making him question everything even more.

He watched Clayton again. Why was the expression on his face so difficult for Ian? He'd known his friend's face for a long time. Yet he looked changed tonight. Finished. Anchored. It rocked Ian to the core.

The band leader said, "May we be joined on the dance floor by the maid of honor and the best man?"

"By the way, I don't know how to dance." Laney put her drink down at a side table, and Ian followed.

"I don't know how to do anything elaborate. It's just that one-two-three, one-two-three bit."

"That you learned at cotillion?"

"Yup. From when I was twelve." More formalities from his youth. Step-two-three, with snobby rich girls, step-two-three. No sex or soul in it, even though his body told him that dancing could have been both a sensual and profound act.

"Heaven help you."

"What I want is right there." The band leader began to sing a popular love song. "We were meant as a pair."

For some unexplainable reason, Ian felt giddy as he and Laney took to the dance floor beside Melissa and Clayton, the eyes of all of the guests on them. Was there something so unusual about Laney that it threw his usual steady equilibrium off? Because when he put his arm at her waist, he felt that something he suspected was out there. Not nothing but something. A serious something.

"Ready?" he asked once they were in position. "And one, two, three, one…"

He continued counting, hoping Laney would find the beat and they could sync into a rhythm.

"I would walk without fear," the band leader crooned, "every moment we share."

"Ouch," he couldn't help but snap his foot back as she stepped hard on his toes.

"Sorry, yeah, yeah." She tried to follow his

movements. It wasn't going well. "Stop pulling on me!"

"I'm not pulling on you. It's called leading. You're supposed to follow me."

"How am I supposed to know what you're doing so I can follow? I can't see your feet."

"You're supposed to move with me."

"Where?"

"Move with my movements. Ow."

Another stab to the top of his foot. He knew Laney didn't mean to be so bad at this, but he couldn't wait for it to be over. This wasn't how it went in the movies.

As she looked at herself in the Ladies Room mirror, Laney was coming unglued. The armpits of her dress had stretched out and were showing under-boob and sweat stains. The circles under her eyes were dark. Unglued mentally and emotionally, too. Everything about this wedding was harder than she had anticipated it was going to be. Being back in Boston. Knowing that the café in Pittsfield was gone. Enrique out of her life, but not without leaving a figurative scar on her psyche. Here in spirit to remind her that fairy tale weddings weren't for her.

Ian wasn't helping matters any. What a disaster dancing, or attempting to dance, with him had been. She didn't know how to dance with a partner and hadn't thought to learn, hadn't considered that would be one of her last-minute maid of honor responsibilities. Instead, she stumbled all over his feet, feeling like a klutz. Plus, he'd spoken of meeting the right sort of woman to marry and all of that, driving it home for the thousandth time that Laney would be no one at this party's consideration. Ian was just like Enrique. Except he wasn't. She couldn't exactly put her finger on it yet, but there was something inside his eyes. A longing that was lingering under the surface, something caught and unable to make itself known yet. It was none of her concern, even though she kept thinking about it. That secret within him haunted her.

"Here. I think our drinks disappeared while we were dancing," Ian said, standing on the sidelines of the reception hall when Laney returned. He handed her a fresh purple Mel-Clay, the silly unimaginative cocktail name for the bride and groom's brew.

As Laney accepted the drink from him, their fingers brushed along the glass's stem during the handoff. An unexpected current sizzled up her finger. She took a grateful sip, thirsty from their dancing fiasco. "If we could call what we did dancing. I'm sorry I stepped on your foot that once."

"It was four times, but who's counting? I'm beginning to get some feeling back in my feet now." They stood watching older people boogie to an upbeat tune. "I take it you haven't done much dancing with a partner?"

"Yeah, that would be none."

"Crackled cauliflower with a sriracha glaze?" A server thrust her tray at them.

"Oh, yes," Laney said while grabbing a crunchy-looking morsel speared on a pick. "I don't know what 'crackled' means, but I'm starving."

Ian picked a spear also. "Me too."

"Yummy. The sauce is spicy, but it's cut with the sweetness in the glaze."

Another server approached. "Melon cubes wrapped in prosciutto?"

"You bet." Ian answered for them both as he grabbed two and two napkins, which were the same emerald green as Laney's dress and Ian's tie and cummerbund.

The corner of the napkin was decorated with a heart that had *M&C* inside of it. Laney wondered what hors d'oeuvres she might have served at the L&E wedding that was never to happen.

"Nice," she said, voting on her bite. "A little balsamic on the melon to contrast the flavors."

"This isn't the city's most renowned wedding venue for no reason."

"Would you like to get married in a swanky place like this? Or are you more the orchard and barn type? Or the tropical island destination wedding?"

Ian laughed. "I haven't got the slightest idea. I don't even know who I'm marrying. She can choose what she wants, no matter to me."

Right after he said that, his eyes clicked to Clayton, who was dancing with Melissa. Laney wondered what Ian was thinking. That all this wedding folderol was nonsense?

"Melissa and Clayton are going to Bermuda tomorrow for their honeymoon. But just the two of them, no wedding party on the beach thing."

The bandleader announced, "Ladies and gentlemen, please return to the tables for dinner."

"We have to be host-y and make sure Melissa and Clayton have everything they need."

Laney rushed to help Melissa and that extra piece of dress, as Ian called it, get properly seated at the sweetheart table, which was placed in the center of the room so that all of the guests could see the bride and groom while they ate, an option Laney thought was a horrible fate. Guaranteeing that if a piece of bread went awkwardly into her mouth, the entire room would see it. But Melissa and Clayton chose to sit on an old-timey orange settee, surrounded by floral displays as if they were in the center of a Victorian garden.

After stepping back once the bride and groom were situated, she said to Ian, "It's sweet. Kind of."

"Clayton told me they were adding some special foods to their menu to make things extra unique. A private label wine. Some kind of elite oysters that come from a small-scale farm. They're supposed to be the finest in the world and cost something like a hundred dollars each."

"I hope they're worth it." They took places next to each other at the wedding party's table. With great formality, he pulled the chair out for her to sit.

She looked at him quizzically.

"What?" he asked.

"Nothing."

"Is there something wrong with pulling a chair out for a lady?"

"It's just so… I'm not used to it."

"Your ex didn't pull a chair out for you?"

"I'm surprised he didn't make me pull his out for him."

Ian frowned. "It sounds like you're better off without him." He made a big gesture of sweeping his hand across the chair. "Mademoiselle."

She giggled.

They ate beef tenderloin with chimichurri sauce and red new potatoes while Laney watched Melissa and Clayton feed each other the hundred-dollar oysters. Laney tried not to be sad. It was a challenge. She'd loved Enrique, or at least loved the idea of him. Why wouldn't she have wanted to move to Madrid with an exciting man and open a café there? They might have had a sweet life, might have had children.

She really didn't want to think about Enrique anymore tonight. So she asked Ian some trivial questions. Favorite food, things about Boston and so on. His mind seemed a million miles away, and he barely answered her questions out of the side of his mouth. She'd be glad when she was done being coupled off with him. He was too hard to read. She spent the rest of the meal listening to the bridesmaid seated on her other side blather about her own recent breakup. Laney couldn't wait to get out of her dress, into a pair of jeans and on with her life.

By the time the grapefruit sorbet course arrived, she needed to get some fresh air, so excused herself and made her way through the cocktail lounge to the outdoor terrace. Slipping through the doors, she took a breath of the warm evening air. She sighed at the nightlights, contemplating what was to be her fate. Would she end up alone, like her mother? Then, surely, being a single parent would be her only option for motherhood. With maybe an accidental pregnancy, or adoption or by using a sperm donor. Maybe that would be okay, like it was for her and her mom. *Relax*, she told herself. Everything didn't have to be figured out this weekend. She'd fall back into her place in the city.

On her fifth deep breath, she heard the terrace door open behind her.

It was Ian. "Oh, you're here, too," he said.

She shook her head. There was no getting away from him.

CHAPTER THREE

"HI."

One of the bridesmaids sidled up to Ian at the bar, where he was having a quiet cordial. Carolyn, Caroline, Carolina… What was her name?

"Hi," he managed to say.

"Do you live in Boston, Ian?"

"Yes. In Back Bay."

"Oh, that's nice." Back Bay was one of the city's most expensive and desirable neighborhoods, with its European flair and great shopping and restaurants. "I'm thinking of moving to town. I'm in West Roxbury with my parents."

"What would be prompting the move?" he asked to continue the conversation. That's what people did, right? Asked questions. Looked for connection points. He needed to start practicing so that he could discern if he liked one woman more than the other. In order for him to choose one, or that they could choose each other and settle down into coupledom. That sounded so bloodless he wanted to scream, but it was his truth. No point fighting it.

The bridesmaid used her pinkie finger to touch one corner of her mouth and then the other. Presumably, she was concerned about her lipstick. "I read you were named one of the city's most eligible bachelors." Based on his family's prominence. "Are you really single, Ian, or are you secretly with someone?" Hmm, that was straightforward. There was certainly nothing immediately apparent that was wrong with Carolyn/Caroline/Carolina. Other than that it felt like pulling teeth to prolong the chitchat. He knew he wasn't out for fireworks, but he at least wanted easy companionship, someone he could be authentic with. That wasn't too outlandish to hope for, was it?

He thought about Laney and a smile came to his face. She was so honest and forthcoming. The way her hair was an utter disaster at the photo shoot before the rehearsal dinner. The way she defiantly didn't want to wear makeup even with the stylist chasing after her. There was something funny and charming about that. Although an impeccable appearance would be required for who-

ever someone of Ian's standing married. The
Luss women managed brains and beauty. His
mother was a tall, cool blonde who never
stepped out of the house unless she was flawless from head to toe.

"You guessed it. I actually am spoken for,"
he lied. There was no reason to hurt her feelings, especially after she'd made herself vul-
nerable. "She is…out of town this weekend."

Carolyn/Caroline/Carolina was a stunning
woman, polished and primped. She didn't
smack of desperation, just practicality, asking if he was truly single. Then he thought of
Laney again, bombing in her wedding speech.
She kept popping into his mind. Where was
she now? After they'd accidentally both tried
unsuccessfully to find solitude on the terrace,
he'd come back inside. Had she?

He supposed it was about time to cut the
cake, and he'd probably be expected to pose
for yet more photos. "I think we're due back
inside."

"I'll be there in a minute," Carolyn/Caro-
line/Carolina said. She'd noticed a couple of
men leaning on the far side of the bar sipping
drinks, so she sauntered over.

Inside the reception hall, the party was
still in full swing. Half the guests were on

the dance floor, and others huddled at the tables attempting to talk over the volume of the music. Melissa and Clayton stood in the center of it all receiving well wishes, their smiles maybe a little strained as the event wore on.

He moved farther into the room and watched an older lady dancing with a teenage boy who looked miserable. Every time he stepped away, the elderly lady yanked him back. When they swung apart again, Ian spotted Laney. She was dancing with a short dark-haired man. Ian had no idea who he was. They weren't touching, however they did seem to be looking into each other's eyes. He couldn't think of a reason to, but he felt jealous. Ian and Laney meant nothing to each other. He had no plans to see her after the wedding. They hadn't even established a cordial best man and maid of honor rapport; it had been prickly. Yet he wanted that man away from Laney—immediately. Which was crazy.

As if possessed by a spirit outside of himself, he moved into the thick of the dance floor to find them. He shimmied his shoulders a little bit as if he were into the groove.

"May I cut in?" he asked when he got close enough.

That was how it was done, wasn't it? It was

an accepted social convention to ask her to excuse herself from dancing with the man and switch to dancing with him.

Maybe it should have been, except that Laney furrowed her brows and said, "Uh, no. I'm dancing with…what was your name?"

"Quincy," the man answered, squirming left and right in his too-tight pants.

"Quincy," Laney repeated to Ian as if he hadn't just heard it.

It was ridiculous that any of this bothered him. Why did he want to swoop Laney into his arms and waltz with her like a prince at a ball? They'd already proven they couldn't dance like that together. Plus, that was the lovey-dovey stuff he was supposedly having no part of. Jealousy and sweeping a woman into his embrace! She'd declined his request to whisk her away, so he had to respect that. Which meant he stood on the dance floor alone, not knowing what to do with himself.

He caught sight of the flower girl, probably all of six-years-old in her matching emerald-green dress. He got her attention and followed the butterfly wing arms she was swirling around with. Ian enjoyed the pure impulsive-ness and had a genuinely carefree few min-utes sharing a giggle with the little girl but he did notice Laney studying him from the corner of her eye.

It was the wee hours before the last of the guests left. Some of the relatives who had traveled great distances were departing in the morning, so Melissa and Clayton pressed on, devoting time to each of them.

"Help me get the gifts onto these carts, and we'll bring them to the bridal suite for the night," Laney said, still ready to pitch in.

Too tired to argue that the wedding manager could call in some staff to do the task, Ian set to it. They stacked the gifts on the cart, larger ones on the bottom. Many were wrapped by the upscale store where Melissa and Clayton had done their registry, so he knew he was attending to thousands upon thousands of dollars' worth of merchandise.

"Home and kitchen goods, of course," Ian said. "That's what couples are given as gifts."

"It makes sense," Laney said. "In older times, when a bride and groom would be moving in together and had never lived alone out of their parents' house, they would need these things."

Ian had been mentally reviewing wedding customs all night. Making notes for his own.

His apartment had a kitchen full of barely used state-of-the-art equipment and appliances. Would he need all new things when he married?

Clayton chatted with some relatives. He'd now switched from ecstatic to something else. Perspiration was beading on his upper lip; in fact, sweat from his brow was running down his face. He must have been exhausted after hours and hours of being *onstage*, as it were. Ian hoped that when he and Melissa got on the plane to Bermuda, they could let their hair down and soak in some much-needed relaxation.

"So, what, you liked dancing with that Quincy guy?" he asked Laney behind the pyramid of gifts.

"What does it matter to you?"

"Not a stitch. Just curious. I thought you were off men."

"I am. It was just something to do. Especially since I was a disaster at dancing with you, the evening got long."

"You just don't know how to dance. You could learn." That image of whirling her around the dance floor popped into his head again.

"Look at Melissa over there." Laney pointed at the bride, who was pale as a ghost as she bid someone farewell. "Her coloring is kind of gray at this point."

"Green, actually," said Ian.

They stood bearing witness as Melissa suddenly put her hand over her stomach.

"Yeah, she doesn't seem right."

"Neither does Clayton." Clayton's face had become red, and sweat had soaked the front of his tuxedo shirt. They turned back to Melissa, whose head rotated in a circle like she was in a daze.

"They can't take much more of this. Should we do something?" said Laney.

Ian and Laney watched Melissa mouth *Excuse me* to her guests and then dash across the reception hall toward the Ladies Room.

"Food poisoning. And judging from the fact that they both have fevers, a bad case of it." The club's on-duty physician was quickly able to piece together a diagnosis.

As the last of the out-of-town relatives had said their goodbyes long after the clock had struck midnight, Melissa and Clayton simultaneously began vomiting in the deserted bathrooms.

"The oysters," Ian said to Laney.

"In August. A month that doesn't have an

R in it." The age-old advice not to eat oysters in warm weather should have been heeded.

"The special menu that only the bride and groom ate."

"Clayton told me they were some kind of rare breed of oysters and cost a hundred dollars each!"

"Money well spent. Not."

"Can we sue the caterer?"

The service lamps were on. No longer were the party lights casting a flattering glow on the guests. The staff had cleared away everything from the last plate to spoon to linen, uncovering the tabletops made from plastic and metal. Ian and Laney sat side by side at one of the long-vacated tables. One of the waiters had been kind enough to provide them with a carafe of coffee and a couple of cups. The doctor promised to check back in a little while.

The bride and groom were now slumped on the settee of their long-planned sweetheart table where they had eaten the offending oysters. Melissa's third dress of the evening, a slinky retro movie-star-type gown that clung to her body, was wet and off-kilter from its many trips to the Ladies Room. Clayton didn't look much better in his untucked and soiled shirt, the tie and jacket long since tossed off. They dabbed their faces with cold washcloths. The sequence that had now repeated itself several times began with one of them making a groaning sound. That was followed with a stomach cramp, quickly followed by a mad dash to the bathroom. After a few minutes, one or the other would return with less of a cry than a whimper as they staggered back to the settee. Then a plop down next to the other.

"I love you Mel," Clayton would manage.

"I love you, too, Clay." Then a groan would come and the steps would be repeated.

"We're supposed to be on the way to our honeymoon in a couple of hours," Melissa said in a labored, scratchy voice.

"The resort in Bermuda is expecting us."

"I can't get on a plane."

"I guess we'll have to postpone." Clayton scrunched his face in distress at the realization.

"The doctor said we probably wouldn't be eating normally again for a week."

"Don't mention food."

"I don't think I've ever felt sicker."

"Ian," Clayton called over to him in a feeble voice. "Can you look up the cancellation procedure for the resort?"

"Of course." He reached for his phone in his tuxedo pants pocket and began.

Laney felt so bad for them. Any bride and groom were probably so looking forward to their honeymoon. To recuperate from all the planning and decisions and details that had gone into their wedding day. Even though it was for different reasons, Laney could relate. How much she'd love to be heading to a resort in Bermuda with its pink sand beaches, clear waters and a luxury resort.

It would surely be nice. Oh, to walk with her toes in the water, taking in the ocean breezes and allowing her mind to clear. She could let go of the past, and physically, mentally and spiritually prepare to start over. Of course, she didn't have the money for an exotic island destination. Nothing like that was in her future. Maybe a walk along the city's Charles River next week.

"Not great news," Ian announced, reading from his phone. "There are no cancellations within forty-eight hours of scheduled arrival. I texted the concierge on twenty-four-hour call, and she apologized but restated their policy."

"Oh, great," Melissa said, sulking. "Not only are we not able to go, we'll lose all of the money we spent. We'd booked a first-class flight, the resort's most lavish villa, private beach, private garden, the whole thing."

Laney figured they could afford to rebook sometime later, but still, it was a terrible shame that such a glorious escapade would go unclaimed.

"Private golf cart," Clayton added.

"Gourmet meals," Melissa threw in.

At the word *gourmet*, Clayton lurched and then made his next dash to the Men's Room.

"Unless anybody needs anything," Ian announced after finishing his coffee, "I'm going to check on Clayton and then head to my room."

Some of the wedding party were staying in the exclusive hotel that occupied the lower five floors of the Fletcher Club, compliments of the groom.

Melissa pouted, "Thank you for everything, Ian. It was a beautiful wedding until… it wasn't."

Laney piped up, trying to be helpful. "It will all make for a memory you'll laugh over with your grandchildren someday."

Ian tilted his head and looked at Laney with a wry smile that somehow shot right into her heart. He lifted his shoulders. "Grandchildren. There's a thought. Goodnight. Or should I say, good morning."

"See you in a few hours," said Laney.

They'd agreed to reconvene and help the newlyweds get packed up and get everything out of the club.

Melissa's head lolled back, so she didn't witness Laney eyeing Ian walk across the reception hall as he left. He confused her. Why did his stare pierce through her at the mention of grandkids? As he'd explained, marriage and breeding for him was just part of an overall corporate strategy. In turn, grandchildren extended the family's master scheme for another generation. The Lusses were a strange breed from what he had told her.

Although, perhaps they had a mentality shared with the uber-rich of the world. Mate with your head, not with your heart. Sound thinking, really. That wasn't her, though. She was all or nothing. Madly in love or totally alone, thank you very much. Yet, there was something so adorable about the way Ian had fluttered butterfly arms with the flower girl while Laney was dancing with Quincy. She couldn't imagine him as a dry and distant father.

Laney had found things complicated when he had tried to cut in on her with Quincy. On principle, she wasn't going to let him decide who she was and wasn't going to dance with. Enrique would have objected, which he did most unsubtly, if he didn't like her interactions with other men. Ian had no right and no cause.

Yet, Laney had to admit how much she liked it when he had tried to take her from Quincy. She'd never let him know, but that made her feel coveted. It wasn't something she'd felt very often, and it tickled her from the roots of her hair to the tippy tops of her toes. She was glad she said no, but she thought she might remember the interaction forever.

And what Ian didn't see later was that Quincy kept trying to hold her by the hips even though they weren't partner dancing. She ended up slipping out of his clutches at the earliest opportunity.

"Laney." Melissa bobbled her head up and spoke in a drunken-sounding voice, no doubt loopy from being sick and awake all night. "I have an idea. Why don't you go to Bermuda and enjoy my honeymoon?" The bride giggled at herself.

"What?" Laney sat down near her.

"The nonrefundable villa in Bermuda. The first-class plane tickets. You should go instead."

"Like I'd just go by myself? To your private villa."

"Yeah, why not? I know that you've been through a lot lately. Couldn't you use the vacation and relaxation?"

Melissa had no idea! She was offering a place where Laney could walk on the beach? To think and sort herself out. To send the hurts of the past ebbing away with the tide. To let sunrises fill her with energy and enthusiasm for starting anew. What an extraordinary offer.

"Are you sure?"

"Why not? What's the point of letting my beautiful honeymoon go to waste?" She frowned.

"You'll reschedule when you're better. You have your whole lives together."

"I know, right? I'm a married lady now."

"You sure are."

"You'll meet your man soon, too. I'm certain of it."

Laney doubted that. "Sure."

"Hey, what time is it?" the disheveled bride asked. "We had an early flight. You'd better hurry. We have a car booked to take us—uh, you, to the airport."

"Are you sure about this?"

"Yeah. It's not like we're going to be able to go."

With the snap of a finger, Laney was headed to a vacation in paradise. She couldn't think of a reason in the world not to say yes to the lovely offer. Well, maybe one. She and Ian were supposed to help Melissa and Clayton get packed up this morning. If she had a plane to catch, she wouldn't be able to complete her maid of honor duties. Obviously, Melissa wouldn't mind. Although it did bother Laney that she wouldn't be seeing Ian again this weekend. Which was absurd and didn't matter in the slightest. Not a bit.

"Again?"

"I can't believe…"

"Yup." Ian scratched his chin as he watched Clayton make another beeline to the bathroom, this time in the honeymoon suite. When Ian had found him lying on towels in the Men's Room in the reception hall, he helped him to the suite and texted Melissa that he'd done so. The groom plunked down on the gold satin linens of the king-size bed where wedding nights continued. Long after the band had finished, the ballroom lights had been dimmed and the aunties had gone home, private celebrations would start. Where a bride and groom, whether it was for the first time or whether they'd been sharing a bed for years, would lay down together as husband and wife. Ian found something ancient and sacred in that, the couple commemorating their legal union with a physical act.

"Some wedding night," Clayton lifted his head. "I'm dizzy, but not in a favorable way. Where's my bride?"

"Last I saw her, she was availing herself of the bathroom in the reception hall. Laney was with her."

Ambling around the suite, Ian stopped to finger the petals of a white long-stemmed rose that stood with eleven others in a beveled vase. The petal felt like velvet, an amazing achievement by Mother Nature. Along with, for example, Laney's luminous light brown eyes. *Wait, what?* He was comparing the wonders of a rose to the eyes of a woman he barely knew and who was no part of his life. He was definitely going cuckoo. He needed a vacation.

"Oh, my wife," Clayton blubbered dramatically into the air, knowing she couldn't hear him, then wiped his face with a wet towel.

Still fingering the flower, Ian asked, "How

did you know Melissa was the right woman for you?"

Ian and Clayton had met at Oxford University and found they both hailed from Boston. They were sons and grandsons of giants, the American elite of the elite. They never heard the word *no*. Even so, they were taught to be honorable people, and they didn't lord their power over women. They didn't have to. Women flocked to them. They posed and paraded around them like display items for sale. That was when Ian realized that finding someone to trust, someone who liked him for him and not only for his family name, wasn't going to be easy. And on the other hand, the life of a Luss wife was what he had to offer, and he did want someone who understood what would and wouldn't be the arrangement.

"I knew Melissa was the one because when I wasn't around her, I wanted to be." Clayton let out a growl at his predicament. "My stomach is killing me!"

"Do you want some water?"

"Definitely not," he answered with a small heave.

"Anyway…" Perhaps it would help to keep Clayton distracted from his discomfort.

"Anyway, when I'm with her, I feel I'm

at my best. Like our hearts are connected. Hopeful. Safe. And what makes it even better is to know I make her feel those things, too."

"When you know, you know?"

"Yeah."

Clayton's family didn't have quite the hard and fast rules about mating that Ian's did. That was okay. Family was family. He was proud that Luss Global Holdings employed hundreds of people who counted on the company's leadership to make smart decisions. "I'm very happy for you, Clayton. Other than the vomiting and all."

At that, he got a comic sneer from his friend. "I know Melissa is going to be disappointed— tomorrow, this morning or whatever the heck time it is—that we're not going to Bermuda."

"You'll reschedule."

"Hey, do you want to go?"

"To Bermuda?"

"Yeah. Use the reservation. Might as well. Otherwise, I'll lose the money."

"Go to the resort?"

"For that matter, you could invite someone if you wanted to. Any female prospects you've encountered lately?"

"No." Ian snickered.

Nothing could be further from the truth.

His grandfather Hugo had been pressuring him to find someone. He wouldn't retire until Ian was settled so that the succession was secured. His son, Rupert, Ian's father, was in Zurich running the international arm of the company. And since Ian's uncle Harley proved himself unable to take over the domestic arm from Hugo, Ian would do it, stepping up from his current position directing appraisals and risk management. Ian would produce children and Luss Global Holdings would continue to grow. All of it outlined and scheduled. In fact, Hugo had already set Ian up on a couple of dates with appropriate women, none to his liking.

Ingrid was a chilly neuroscience researcher at Massachusetts General Hospital. During the two dates they went on, she spoke of nothing but her work, using terms like *basolateral amygdala* and *temporal lobe structure*. He was impressed with her distinguished career, but he thought she'd be better suited with someone in a similar field. He had to have *something* he could talk about with his mate.

Thea was part of a family like Ian's, whose domination in their field, of manufacturing plastic goods, made them a massive fortune. With dark hair and thick, busy eyebrows, she was a numbers cruncher, and there were three guests at their dinner together. Ian, Thea and her the calculator app on her phone. She showed Ian one financial scenario after the next, if they were to expand into India. This set of numbers if they forged into Africa. By the time dessert arrived, Ian's eyes were rolling back in his head. He didn't need a wife who exhausted him. The search wasn't going to be easy.

"So go on your own," Clayton suggested. "You could probably use a vacation. When was the last time you traveled when it wasn't for work?"

Clayton had him there. Why shouldn't he take a little time off and just walk on a beach alone? He could think about how he was going to know what woman was right for him. Someone who could really go the distance under their family's rules but who he could live contentedly with.

Ian's mother and father did. Vera was involved in her charities, in her case raising money for women's groups in war-torn areas of the world. His mother also had her female friends who met for lunch and cocktails and shopping all over Europe. She and Ian's dad had that cordial, serviceable and supportive relationship that the Luss family required. Everyone understood what was expected of them, and it all fit together like a puzzle.

His grandmother told him something else, words that spoke to him in the dark of night, but that was beside the point.

Warm sand under his feet and the notifications on his phone set to Off sounded pretty nice.

"Okay," he tilted his head so it was in line with Clayton's. "Thanks. I'll go."

"Great. We booked an early flight, so you'll need to head out soon."

"You know, the maid of honor and I were supposed to supervise getting your gifts and clothes and whatnot rounded up and out. I'll be leaving that all to Laney." That stuck in his craw. He'd not only renege on his duty but miss the chance to spend a little more time with her. She somehow exasperated and intrigued him at the same time with her sincerity and frankness. *Oh, well.* It couldn't be helped.

"Don't worry about it. My mom or Melissa's mom will deal with it. They live for that sort of thing."

"Well then, I guess I'm on my way to your honeymoon."

CHAPTER FOUR

IT WAS ALL happening so fast. A chauffer in full uniform held open the door of a shiny black stretch limo in front of the Fletcher Club. Laney had never been in a limo and slid into the soft leather of the back seat, swinging her legs in after her as glamorous as a movie star. After making sure she was comfortably situated, the driver gently closed the door.

Take that, Enrique. As she had told Ian, Enrique never held a door open for her, always leaving her standing in the cold as he first let himself into a car, sometimes putting on sunglasses or taking off a scarf before he bothered to click the button that opened the passenger door. She never knew whether he was like that with all women, himself the golden child whose mother thought he walked on water, or whether he didn't deem Laney worthy of the chivalrous treatment.

He thought he was *slumming it* with her; he made that clear. Why she was dumb enough to think he'd fall in love with her and none of that would matter, she had no idea. Wishful thinking. Lesson learned.

As the limo pulled away, the driver informed her, "Ma'am, in the tray in front of you, you'll find coffee, freshly squeezed orange juice and a bucket of champagne on ice. There's also fruit and warm croissants. Is there anything else you'll need?"

"No," she choked out, trying to keep from laughing. "That ought to do it, thank you."

Of course, she didn't need more than that just to make it the short distance to the airport. She'd had coffee to keep herself awake while she hastily gathered up her belongings in order to catch the flight. She left the formal bridal party clothes behind. Melissa assured her that the resort in Bermuda had shops where she could pick up beach and casual clothes and whatever she needed. In fact, the honeymoon reservation included a generous shopping allowance.

At the airport, the driver pointed out to her where to go in the terminal, and from there, she was ushered straight into the first-class lounge, where a pink-suited attendant welcomed her. Melissa had been able to text her travel agent and get the name changed on the reservation. "I'm Serena from Pink Shores Resort. Will your significant other be joining you shortly?" Laney's mouth opened wide as if to answer, but no words came out. Significant other? She didn't know what this woman was talking about. "While you're waiting, perhaps you'd like a light breakfast. Coffee, freshly squeezed orange juice, champagne, fruit and warm croissants."

"Thank you."

The exact same menu the limo driver had offered. Hmm, that wasn't a half bad way to live! After all, there could never be too many buttery pastries in the world. Although she politely declined, having already gobbled two in the limo. Her rest and reset was getting off to a delicious start.

Boarding began. The first-class cabin was appointed with huge reclining chairs. Laney's was by the window, the one beside it vacant, no doubt the two seats that had been assigned to Melissa and Clayton. Laney began exploring the amenities for the two-hour flight. The headrest behind her was so plush she could sink right into it. A partition offered privacy. She had her own extra-large touch screen to watch whatever she wanted on the personal entertainment center. She flipped through the channels, ranging from first-run movies to hit television shows to live sporting events to dozens of types of music. Padded headphones were provided as well as the latest technology in earbuds. There was an e-reader loaded with hundreds of books. A pull-out tray was positioned for comfortable laptop use or for eating. There was a lighting panel with many options. The flight attendant offered never-used blankets and pillows for her comfort.

"We'll be departing shortly," Serena popped her head in. "Has your companion encountered a delay?"

Laney didn't know what to say or do. Since Melissa hadn't brought it up, she figured she'd just board the plane without any questions. She noticed that Serena was careful to use the words *companion* and *significant other*, not saying any names out loud for privacy and not making any gender assumptions.

"I'll try to reach him, but he'll take another flight if need be," she said, quickly fudging.

"As you know, Pink Shores Resort is a couples-only retreat."

Wait, what?

"We maintain our reputation as a five-star,

world-renowned romantic destination by enforcing our protocol. We ask our couples to arrive and depart together."

"I'll call him right now." After Serena moved on, Laney called Melissa in a panic.

"Oh no!" Melissa shrieked in a still-woozy voice. "I didn't know the resort had that exclusivity."

"What should I do now? I lied and said my significant other was on his way. And then I said he was taking another flight."

"I'm so sorry. Maybe if you can just get to Bermuda, I'll call them and explain."

"Didn't Ian do that last night?" He'd relayed to the group the inflexibility of the booking restrictions.

"I'm sorry, Ms. Sullivan," Serena poked around the partition again. "The captain would like to prepare for take-off. As I mentioned, we only allow our resort's couples on the flights. We'll have to ask you to deplane along with me, and then we'll gladly get you onto the next flight once your significant other has arrived. Perhaps you'd enjoy a croissant while you wait. Kindly follow me."

There went her ritzy vacation. That was Laney's luck. Nothing had gone right for her. Not Enrique. Not the café. Not even her interactions with the best man, Ian, this weekend. Now this.

With a resigned exhale, Laney rose. Embarrassed, she looked around at her fellow passengers in the first-class section, which seemed to be filled with Pink Shores Resort guests, based on an identifying tag clipped on the side of their seats. They were, indeed, all couples. Newlyweds and those who looked like they were commemorating milestone anniversaries. Maybe a twenty-fifth. Maybe even a fiftieth. Couples of mixed races, same-sex pairs, all whispering to each other or holding hands or leaning over to give one another a kiss. United in one solitary purpose. Excitedly on their way to celebrate their love. Laney felt horribly out of place.

As she reached down to grab her bag and then get off the plane, she heard a familiar male voice. "There was an accident on the highway that delayed my arrival to the airport."

Where did she know that voice from? She'd heard it recently. Whose was it?

"We're glad you made it," came Serena's voice. "Have a pleasant flight."

Bag in hand, Laney stood and turned to see who was rushing down the aisle.

No, no, no, no!

It was Ian! She sat back down.

The pilot announced over the sound system, "Flight crew, lock the doors for departure."

Ian slipped into the seat that the flight attendant had gestured to and swiveled his chair to face front. He observed that the occupant of the seat next to him had a shapely pair of legs. When he followed the legs up, he did a double take. It couldn't be.

"Laney?"

"What are *you* doing here?" she retorted.

"What are *you* doing here?"

"Melissa invited me."

"Clayton insisted I use the vacation so it didn't go to waste. Everything was prepaid and nonrefundable."

"Please fasten your seat belts for takeoff," a flight attendant instructed Ian, who pulled the strap to comply.

"I know, I was in the room when you called to try to explain the situation. Melissa wanted *me* to use the reservation."

"Without telling Clayton?"

"When you're lying down on the bathroom floor, perhaps you don't do your best thinking."

"Clayton was in about the same shape."

"Apparently, they didn't tell either of us that Pink Shores Resort is for couples only. The resort's representative was about to make me leave because I was onboard without my significant other."

Ian quickly called Clayton before he needed to turn off his cell phone. "Hey, thanks for the invite, but did you know that the resort is couples only? And did you know that Laney is on the plane? That Melissa told her to use the reservation."

"What? No. Melissa, did you…? Let me put you on speakerphone, she's right here."

"Melissa?" Laney brought her mouth close to the phone.

"Yeah." Ian switched the speaker on, and Melissa's voice came through. "Clay and I are lying in bed together, still in half of our wedding clothes. Honey, you texted the travel agent and put Ian on the reservation?"

"I forgot to tell you."

"Can we make some other arrangement with the resort?" Laney piped in. "The rep here told me we have the honeymooners' villa."

Ian asked, "Do you think we could swap it for two smaller rooms?"

"Just go and have a nice time," Clayton said.

"I'm sure the villa is big enough that you won't even see each other."

There was nothing to be done. Ian knew he had about one minute to make his objection known, disrupt the flight and force his way off the plane. If he didn't, he'd be spending the week with Laney. She of the café au lait eyes and the bum luck of late.

"I guess we're on our way, then."

"I guess so." She pursed her lips, maybe as unsure about this as he was.

"I've got to get in one more call before the captain insists we shut our electronics down." He tapped his speed dial for a number he used frequently, although he turned off the speaker. "Grandfather."

"Where are you, Ian? It sounds like you're on an airplane."

"Yes, I'm on a commercial flight." Luss Global had its own jet and, if it was occupied, Ian would generally hire a private plane. "I just wanted to let you know that I'm taking a quick holiday to Bermuda."

"All right. But I want you to know that I've been speaking with colleagues, and I'm going to be gathering the names of some more women I want you to have dinner with as soon as you get back. And I need you to give each your serious consideration."

Ian glanced over to Laney, who was thumbing through a magazine. He was glad she wasn't hearing Hugo. The matchmaking was so old-school, it was a little humiliating, if efficient. He didn't like the frailty he heard in his grandfather's voice. After a long and prosperous career, and having lost his wife a couple of years ago, it really was time for him to step down. Ian knew he would stick to his word and not do so until his grandson found a bride. It was all on him.

"I will, grandfather."

The Luss marriage rulebook dated back to Hugo's grandfather, Frederick. He would be Ian's great-great-grandfather. Frederick was to partner with his brother Phillip to buy land using the inheritance that their father had left them, plus money they'd earned. Then Phillip met a wily woman who he fell madly in love with. He worshipped the ground she walked on. She told him that her family had forged south to Georgia, and that was where he should purchase the land. Phillip was too blinded by his love for the persuasive woman to cross his t's and dot his i's, and before he knew it, the land had been bought in the woman's name only, a result of her dishonest relatives brokering the sale. Phillip's half of the investment in the new venture with his brother was gone, and the woman disappeared.

After that, Frederick decided that unions between men and women would become trade agreements, mutually beneficial to all parties, with both families thoroughly scrutinized. The process worked well for several generations until Ian's Uncle Harley fell for a party girl, Nicole, a baroness of all things, who should have fit the bill. That was a disaster, and Harley's globe-trotting and reckless spending cost the company tens of millions of dollars. He knew his grandfather wouldn't loosen the reins after that.

"Ladies and gentlemen," the pilot instructed, "we're pulling out of the gate. Please turn off all of your devices or set them to Airplane Mode."

As Ian did, he gazed over at Laney again. He'd spent more time with her at the wedding than he probably had with any woman in ages, if ever. Now he'd be at a faraway resort with her.

"So, what, we have to pretend to be a couple?"

"Not only that, but because we have the

honeymoon villa, we have to pretend to be newlyweds. In public, that is."

He'd never been part of a couple. Even with a cold contract sort of marriage, he'd still have to have some husbandly skills that a woman would want. This could be practice for him. Sure, Laney wasn't the pedigreed type he was expected to marry, but that didn't mean he couldn't masquerade at it with her.

"Is that okay with you? We'll act like we're together when we're out and about at the resort?"

"It sounds kind of wacky, but sure. It seems to mean a lot to Clayton and Melissa that the trip doesn't go to waste."

"Maybe if they feel better, they'll actually decide to come in a few days. And then we'll leave."

They were not going to become fixtures in each other's lives. It was only for a week at most. There was no reason for this not to work out. Perhaps it was fortuitous. It was a chance for Ian to prepare for the next phase of his life. When he accepted Clayton's offer to use the reservation, one of his first thoughts had been that in leaving, he wouldn't get to say goodbye to Laney. In a way, a best man and maid of honor are almost thrown together as a couple. There had already been cheek-to-cheek photos, pulling out chairs, commiserating about speeches and calamitous dancing.

Once the plane was in the air and had reached cruising altitude, the flight attendant approached with a tray. "Can I offer you a cup of fish chowder, a Bermudian favorite, or perhaps you'd like an omelet?"

"I'd love to try the chowder," said Laney. "I love eating like a local."

Ian smiled. "I'll have the same."

He liked that Laney was open to trying interesting food. That was something they could do together on this trip. Plus, as Clayton said, the honeymoon villa was likely to be large. They could each claim their own space and spend the whole week apart if they wanted to. Which he didn't. He wanted to act like he was on his honeymoon. Still, that there were options was a comfort.

The attendant laid cream-colored linen place mats onto their dining trays. She then added a matching napkin and silver utensils. Placing the soup tureens carefully, she presented them with a bread basket filled with warm rolls and a pot of butter.

"What else can I get you to drink?" she asked after also serving glasses of water with ice.

"I'll have a coke," Laney ordered.

"Sparkling water with lime," said Ian.

After a sip, Ian peered across the aisle to study an older couple. They were both holding stemmed glasses that looked to contain red wine. First, they clinked glasses as in a basic toast. Then, without either of them saying anything, they intertwined their arms to feed each other a sip from their own glass. That was followed by a knowing smile, and then the woman leaned closely toward the man and affectionately rubbed her cheek on his shoulder. Ian would bet that they had been together a long time, that there was so much between them that didn't need saying aloud.

"Mrs. Luss."

"What?" Laney looked up from her soup.

"Excellent. I was practicing to see if you'd answer to your new name."

"I don't have to take your name just because we're 'married.'" She made air quotes with her fingers.

"Why don't we just keep it simple and traditional? Less explaining."

"Okay, Mr. Luss. Have you tried the soup, husband? It's delicious."

She helped herself to another spoonful of the chowder, chunky with fish and aromatic vegetables. Then she broke off a piece of the warm roll and swirled it into the soup. Ian expected her to eat it. Instead, she surprised him by popping the bite into his mouth. He fumbled in surprise and then had to lick his lips to make sure all of it made it in.

"That's something couples would do, don't you think?" she said.

A shiver ran down his spine, which was a surprise, ignited by her supple fingers touching his lips with the food morsel. He bunched his forehead, almost annoyed that a couple of fingertips could have such an effect on him. And that wasn't the first time her touch had aroused him. That was the only hitch about spending a week with Laney. She stirred him up. Magic fingers creating involuntary muscle tingles was precisely what he wasn't going to marry, so he surely didn't need to train at it. Or maybe it was that he did need to. To get those longings out of his system, once and for all, so that he could turn his back on them and get on with the future he'd planned.

Hmm. "We should agree on a common story about how we met. Things people might ask."

"Three years ago at a wedding. How about that?"

"You were a bridesmaid and I asked everyone if they knew you. And whether you were seeing anyone."

"Aw, that's cute."

It was at that. He continued, "I noticed you up at the altar in a godawful yellow poofy dress. During the ceremony, you sensed me looking at you, and our eyes met. It wasn't just your beauty, it was your essence, the way you had about you."

"I wanted to stare into your eyes until eternity."

"You hit me like a thunderbolt. I knew you were the one for me. That you'd be the woman I'd marry."

Was he reciting lines from a movie he'd seen or a book he'd read? How else would all of that have come spilling out? Truthfully, he liked the story, liked the notion of love at first sight. Of souls igniting. Knowing in an instant that two people had been put on Earth for each other.

He glanced over to the older couple again. The man brought his wife's hand to his lips so that he could kiss the top of it. His blue eyes crinkled with gratitude.

A lump formed in Ian's throat.

"Welcome, honeymooners." A concierge in a pink jacket met Laney and Ian as soon as they arrived to the Pink Shores Resort. "I am Adalson, and the staff and I are at your service. On behalf of all of us, may we say congratulations on your nuptials, and we wish you a long and happy life together."

Very nice well-wishes after such a momentous milestone of getting married. Had she actually gotten married, that was. In fact, she was never going to get married. At twenty-eight and after Enrique, that was settled. And certainly not to the devastatingly handsome man next to her, who she barely knew.

"Yes, I'm a lucky man," Ian fake-boasted as he tried to lope his long arm around her so they could co-acknowledge Adalson's words. Except that Laney spontaneously jumped back and away from the swerve of his reach. Which left him hugging air. He stuttered, out of context, "We're the Lusses."

Adalson gave them both a confused look. "Perhaps it was a trying flight? Please look forward to relaxing Bermy style."

"Oh yeah, right," she mumbled and corrected herself by stepping into Ian's wingspan.

He gripped her by the shoulder and pulled her in. She managed an inane grin, like her man was just so cute. Then she immediately had to *not* concentrate on how firm his hand on her was. She also had to *not* concentrate on the sturdy side of his body that was meeting hers. *Not* concentrate on how amazing he felt, holding her warm and tight, and how she melted against him. *Not* replay in her mind bringing that bite of chowder-soaked bread to his mouth when they were on the plane. She shouldn't have made such an intimate move in the first place, but he didn't have to turn it into something so sensual. Then the way she could only gawk as he licked his lips. This masquerade was already a challenge. And they'd just arrived.

"We'll bring your bags to your villa. Would you like to walk there on the beach or take a golf cart?"

"Beach," Laney answered.

"Golf cart," Ian blurted in unison, his voice on top of hers.

"I'm sorry, I meant golf cart," she said, trying again.

Right as Ian corrected with "Beach."

They looked at each other and fake-laughed. "Ha ha, ha ha."

Adalson again averted his eyes for discretion, clearly not knowing what to make of them.

Neither did Laney, other than that her head

was starting to spin. Maybe this trip wasn't going to be as easy as it seemed.

"I think you may be a bit tired," Adalson interjected. "Why don't I take you in the cart, and you'll have plenty of occasions to walk on the beach later? That is, if you choose to leave the villa at all."

All three of them knew what he meant. If Laney was the blushing bride type, now would be the time. She wasn't, so she looked lovingly up to her husband, as any happy new wife would.

Adalson drove them along a path that cut through the vibrant green lawn.

"Oh my gosh!" Laney exclaimed when they rounded the corner that allowed them to face the shoreline.

"What?" Ian asked.

"The water is truly turquoise." Exactly like it was in the photos she researched online before she boarded the flight. She didn't know anything about Bermuda, and suddenly she was here. "And the sand. It really is pink."

It seemed like a minute ago that she could only stand idly by while firefighters tried in vain to salvage the café that was blazing away right before her very eyes. Now she was on an island in the middle of the Atlantic Ocean trying to fathom how sand could actually be pink.

"I'm amazed by it every time I come."

Oh, of course the rich guy had been here before. His family probably owned the island. Which didn't stop her jaw from hanging open at the stunning colors of the water and sand. She'd never seen anything like it in her life. It was incredible. She couldn't wait to take her first walk. She'd bet the sand was soft and would feel magical between her toes. And unlike what Adalson was insinuating, it wasn't as if she was going to be inside the whole time with her groom. She was going to be out on the beach and in the water.

"We're getting farther and farther away from the central buildings of the resort," she said to Ian as they rode through a grove of trees and into a secluded area.

"We've entered your private grounds. You have this entire beach to yourself. There's no access other than for you and staff," Adalson explained, "who will text you before entering your villa compound. So please consider this clothing optional."

"Uh-uh," Ian made a noise she couldn't interpret.

What she did understand, however, is the

way the low timbre of his voice sent a hum right through her body. Clothing was going to be mandatory, not optional, around him. This little charade could become dangerous if she didn't protect herself. She couldn't withstand any more hurt. That wasn't what happened on *fake* honeymoons, anyway.

"This is your personal patio and garden." Adalson gestured.

A wooden deck with a white table and chairs, as well as two loungers, were positioned to enjoy a garden. Trees both short and tall swayed in the gentle breeze. A rainbow of flowers grew along a path. Which gave way to the entrance to the villa.

"Our finest and most luxurious accommodations at the resort."

"Wow," said Laney.

It was a house on a beach right at the shore, elevated from the water. The one-story building was painted pastel pink with white trim and a white roof, as was typical Bermudian style. Once Laney and Ian got out of the cart and approached the entrance, she could see that there was a wraparound balcony with a railing made of wooden slats.

"Three hundred and sixty degrees of balcony," Adalson confirmed. "Is that to your liking, ma'am?"

"It certainly is."

"So that you can take in sunrises and sunsets from whatever angle you choose." Ah, as if she might have to settle for only one panoramic view of the sea and sky. "May I show you inside?"

Ian thought quickly to grab her hand as people romantically involved might do. She liked his big palm with its thick fingers. Enrique had slender hands that, to be honest, she never enjoyed holding. He went for frequent manicures, and his hands were always powdery. She liked Ian's; they were strong and manly.

The kind of hand she might like to hold for the rest of her life.

Not Ian's, specifically. Of course.

She'd hold no man's hand until eternity.

Anyway, she was getting flustered in her own thoughts.

The point being that his hand felt good.

"Melissa and Clayton pulled out all the stops for this."

Ian squeezed her palm as a reminder. "I mean, our travel agents did well for us, honey. Didn't they?"

"They did, my beloved."

The beach-facing section of the balcony was a stunner. From French doors that opened into the house, there was a wide white staircase with white bannisters that led straight down into the water. A staircase into the ocean! All they had to do was descend the steps.

"This will do," Ian declared. Then he winked at Laney.

How could a wink feel like a kiss?

CHAPTER FIVE

ENTERING THE VILLA, Ian first thought the aisle of bright red on the floor between the two white sofas was an odd strip of carpeting. Once he got closer, he saw that it was rose petals. Thousands upon thousands of red rose petals created a pathway across the spacious living room.

"There are so many." Laney bent down and scooped up a handful. Bringing them to her nose, she took an exaggerated inhale and exhale. "Mmm."

"If you'll follow the roses—" Adalson gestured "—they'll take you to the newlywed master suite."

Ian managed a close-lipped smile while his stomach hopped. He hadn't had a chance to figure out what they were going to do for sleeping arrangements. Not knowing the other had invited a replacement, neither Melissa nor Clayton had any suggestions. Ian would work something out on how to split up the use of the villa later.

He followed Laney along the rose-petal trail through the next set of French doors, which were symmetrically in line with the set that led to the balcony and staircase into the ocean, all in a row to create a private aisle to the water. His eyes beheld the end of the rose petal trail at the foot of the king-size bed with its four-poster frame and gauzy curtains strung from every side. On top of the bed, many more thousands of red petals formed a gigantic heart atop the lavender-colored bedding. He looked at Laney. She looked at him. In each other's eyes, they almost panicked at the prospect of this giant bed.

Laney covered nicely with a phony yawn. "It's been a long day. I think I'd like to take a little nap before exploring the resort."

Adalson responded, "Ah, yes. Of course. Let me bring in your bags. A member of the housekeeping staff will be by to go over your needs. All of the concierges are available to help you plan activities or sightseeing."

He took his leave and returned with each of their small suitcases, as they'd come with only what they'd brought to the wedding.

There hadn't been time for either of them to go home to pack additional bags.

Adalson put the two cases down. "Mr. Luss, I'm so sorry, there must have been a mix up. I will track down the rest of your luggage and have it brought to you immediately. I'm so terribly sorry."

"No, that's okay. That's all we brought."

Adalson tried to hide his surprise.

"We pack light. Like you said, Adalson," Laney said, jumping in. "We won't need many clothes. It's our honeymoon, after all!"

Ian's eyes popped wide and he mashed his lips together.

"Ah," Adalson nodded his head knowingly, although still doing a double-take at the two small wheelies he'd delivered. "I'll... Congratulations again."

He finally departed, and both Ian and Laney stuck out their tongues in relief.

The layout of the villa was clear. There was one enormous master bedroom with en suite showers, bathtubs and every amenity. There was a living room, sun room, dining room and kitchen, everything done in the finest materials with great detail. There were all of the private outdoor areas. What there wasn't was a second bed of any kind. Of course not. This was a honeymoon villa.

This wasn't a problem. All Ian wanted was to enjoy some time away to become mentally prepared to find a wife. So he could sleep on the floor, on the sofa, out on the balcony— it didn't matter. He and Laney would masquerade as husband and wife in front of other people. Which he still didn't mind the idea of, because it would give him some rehearsal at being a couple, the way he would present himself to the world as a married man.

Although when he saw Laney kicking off her shoes and floating from one open window to the next to take in the views, a longing washed through him. Maybe he wanted more than to playact at love for a week on an island far from his family. Maybe he wanted that connection that true lovers had. That way the older man on the plane cherished his white-haired love. They had something bottomless and profound between them. Something that would last forever, even into eternity. Maybe he wanted to experience those feelings, just once. Despite all of his party-line speak.

"Come see this bathroom," Laney called out, having made her way into the en suite.

"I mean, look at this. The glassed-in shower is big enough for two elephants!"

"Interesting image."

"It has not one, not two, but eight water jets. Imagine how that would feel spraying onto your body."

No sirree, eight water jets spraying him was not going to be a smart thing for him to imagine. That sounded far too sensual. And he was definitely not going to imagine being in the shower with *her*, seeing what those curves he hadn't stopped admiring would look like wearing nothing but eight sprays of water. Much safer to picture two elephants getting extremely clean.

"What do you want to do?" Laney asked as she sauntered around the villa.

"Do?" Ian raised an eyebrow.

"Yeah, do you want to go into the ocean or check out some of the activities in the main buildings? There are lots of ways we could spend our time."

"I think newlyweds usually find something to do on their honeymoon, don't you?"

"Okay. Let's go in the water." She could cool off from the overheated feeling she got thinking about things she wasn't going to do with him.

"That sounds marvelous."

"Except I don't have a bathing suit," said Laney.

There was obviously not any swimming intended during Melissa and Clayton's city wedding weekend, so she'd had no reason to pack one.

"I don't, either."

Laney wasn't going to repeat what Adalson had said about the privacy of their lodgings making clothing optional. She was already sensing the weirdness of being in this villa with him separated from Boston by a lot of ocean. Pretending to be a couple. Clothes were staying on. She'd bet Ian would look incredible with optional clothing off, but nothing like that was going to be happening.

"Let's walk up to the resort shops to buy some, and we can check out the property while we're at it," Ian said.

"I could use some casual clothes, too," Laney said. She didn't have shorts or sandals or a cover-up.

"We'll have to make it a little bit of a spree then."

Shopping spree with Ian Luss. *Hmm.* That

was a turn of events she would have never expected. Why not, though? They both knew the real score.

"Melissa said there was some kind of shopping allowance."

"Or I can buy you a bikini, for heaven's sake."

Suddenly, it occurred to her how self-conscious she'd be in a bathing suit around Ian. At the wedding, he'd commented on her hair, her lack of makeup, a spot on her dress. Although she could tell he'd only meant well, that was a trigger for her, made her feel like it was Enrique all over again, her short curvy body being measured against the tall skinny goddesses of the world. Maybe Ian would have the class to only think insulting thoughts about her body, not need to say them out loud like Enrique did.

She could still hear his voice. *That dress does nothing for your lumps.* Lumps. Not curves. Unattractive lumps.

The center of the resort was comprised of five buildings painted the signature pink and white, and grouped around a mosaic fountain. Guests, indeed in couples, not a single person alone or with children, passed to and fro. The shopping plaza had a row of establishments.

One with mannequins in the window modeling several types of swimsuits from practical styles for water sports to high-fashion bikinis.

Laney decided she would love one of those suits that had a matching cover-up. That would make her feel like a chic bride indeed. Oh, wait, she wasn't that. But, hey, she could have some fun.

As they browsed the store, Ian quickly grabbed a couple of selections, the men's swimsuits much more basic than the women's. Laney picked out a couple of the ensembles like she had in mind and proceeded to the fitting room to try them on. The first one was a modest top and bottom with plenty of coverage, the fabric a sort of ocean motif that had a dark blue, a lighter blue and a white pattern. The cover-up that went with it was styled akin to a man's shirt, buttons all the way down to the hem below knee length. She wasn't sure if she liked it or not. Ian was going to have to see her in these bathing suits at one point or another, so she decided to bite the bullet and poked out of the fitting room to summon his opinion.

"That's…" he stopped himself and she watched his Adam's apple bob as he looked her over from head to toe "…very nice."

She loved that he stumbled over his words. She could tell from his hooded eyelids and the lift to the corners of his mouth that he liked what he saw, that she wasn't getting the Enrique disapproval. She prickled under his observation, shoulders arching closer together. It was a strange turn-on the way he eyed her with a sort of appreciation, as if he were enjoying a leisurely and satisfying scrutiny.

"I don't need to put on makeup or have my hair done?" Her retort was snappy and defensive, harkening back to his comments at the wedding. Here, he didn't have any idea what she was referring to. Flustered, she covered with, "What do you think?"

"You look gorgeous. But shall we compare it to something else before you decide?"

Gorgeous. "Sure."

The next ensemble was far bolder. Solid black, the cut of the top covered much less skin than the first one. The bottoms were certainly more revealing than any she'd ever worn before, basically two triangles tied together on the sides. The sheer crepe kimono that flowed over it made her feel womanly and, well, just plain sexy. She strode toward Ian, whose face froze except for his mouth, which literally dropped open.

She would remember the moment until her dying day. Here she was with Ian Luss, who could have any woman in the world, and he was beaming at her like she was the most enticing creature he'd ever seen. In his gaze she, indeed, felt gorgeous.

It had been cumulative, the way Enrique made her feel not up to par, not attractive enough to keep him from ogling other women. Ian made her feel desirable, which had been hurtful to go so long without. She knew he'd go on to choose one of those classic beauties that billionaires married. But she'd always have today.

Unless…maybe he was just pretending at this, too. Playing the role of the lovestruck husband. He'd be too polite to let her know.

"Please get that," he said, stuttering in a way that made her giggle. He did, too.

Suddenly insecure, she wrapped the kimono tightly around her and cinched the belt. "I'll just buy a couple of these athletic suits," she said and pointed to a rack of high-neck one-piece suits in black and navy. "Maybe I'll be doing some water sports this week."

"Oh, okay, but you're buying the two you just tried on, as well."

"Why?"

He gave her another one of those crooked half-smiles that might make her faint if he kept them up. "Why, wifey, because you look so hot in them."

Now it was her turn to swallow hard. She wasn't sure if he'd just called her wifey because he wanted to remind her that this was phony talk. Since *Ian* should not say things to *Laney* like Mr. Luss would say to Mrs. Luss. In any case, he could have gotten away with not saying anything. He chose to, making her think that he wasn't just playacting. Picking out expensive items at a resort shop and having a handsome, refined man pay her compliments. Yes, this could be an excellent bridge from where she came from to where she was going. It was also the most fun shopping she'd ever had.

After they bought a few more things, Ian had the bags sent to the villa, and they walked past the shopping gallery to a glass atrium filled with tropical plants. In an open area at the center, couples were dancing to a quartet that played a classic love song.

"They're doing lessons," Laney said, observing an older man walking around the couples making corrections.

He lifted a man's arm just so, adjusted the

distance another couple were standing from each other. Laney reflected on the awkward and uncomfortable dancing the two of them did as best man and maid of honor.

"That's what I could have used before the wedding."

The teacher spotted them spying on the ten or so couples who were involved in the class. He approached. "Don't tell me. Your first dance as husband and wife wasn't all you had hoped?"

Close enough to the truth, they both nodded.

"I am Hans. Please join us. This class is for couples who want to know the pleasures of partner dancing."

Ian and Laney looked at each other. She shrugged, "I know you already know how."

"But not with my wife." He held out his arm for her to take it. "May I have this dance?"

"Remember, partners," Hans called out, "in ballroom dancing, one of you is the leader."

"That didn't go well for me last time," Laney said to Ian as the dance instructor guided them into the center of the atrium.

"Here's your chance to learn."

"Leaders," Hans addressed the couples,

"hold your partner at the waist. You do not push or pull. When the leader moves, the partner will naturally respond so that you keep your hold. One hand on the leader's shoulder. Join your other hands. And it's one, two, three…one, two, three…one, two, three…" Hans demonstrated with an invisible partner.

How nimble the elder gentleman was. Ian imagined he'd had a lifetime of dancing, and it was what kept him healthy and young at heart. Hans waltzed himself around to check on the other students. One younger couple were already sashaying all over the dance floor. Two middle-aged men were not so lucky, as they kept looking at their feet and couldn't get a rhythm going.

Ian and Laney made an attempt to get started.

"You're not supposed to come that close," she said, objecting when Ian put his arm around her waist and brought her toward him.

"You're right. We're supposed to keep the frame."

He backed away and tried again. He knew the basics of ballroom dancing, as his parents did, in fact, enroll him in lessons. Right now, though, he was having trouble maintaining his distance for this formal style. He wanted to bring Laney close, to feel her silky hair against his cheek, which he'd had a hint of in between her stepping on his toes at the wedding. To feel her luscious curves against his body again. The hills and valleys that had just been on glorious display when she was trying on those bathing suits.

The mere thought of that gave his body a jolt and he fumbled over his own feet. *Goodness!* That was taking the charade a little too far. All of this with Laney didn't feel completely fake, and that was terrifying. She brought up something from the very depths of him. Something lethal because of its power.

As she began to find it easier to follow his steps, an almost visible energy passed back and forth between them. A spark. His pulse sped up as he worried it was the very force that he needed to avoid. He imagined all sorts of green lights when he knew there were only red flags.

Like if Laney was really his bride, the first thing he would have done upon arrival to the villa would have been to pick her up in his arms and lay her down on that heart full of rose petals atop the bed. He'd brush his lips against hers, ever so lightly, leaving the tiniest space for air to pass between them. At first.

Then he'd caress the side of her face with his palms, learning the creaminess of her skin. He'd probably dot more wispy kisses all over her face. Until his lips returned to hers. This time his kisses would be more urgent. He'd let them tell her what was brewing inside of him. The passion that was going to erupt, that would blow those rose petals off the bed and leave them scattered all over the room. Because once he got his tongue...

He chuckled at himself in disbelief of where his mind and, judging from the sudden change in comfort of his trousers, lower down on his body had traveled to.

Get ahold of yourself, Mr. Luss!

He concentrated only on dancing. As he and Laney got more and more comfortable, he was swept into it, as if together they transcended space and time. As if they glided until their feet didn't even touch ground anymore. He loved the possibility. There was something so beautiful and timeless about it, two people's movements becoming a dance as one. The melding of bodies with music was such a lovely manifestation of their union. He was on cloud nine as he waltzed Laney all around the dance floor. Like another scene from a movie. Dancing around the room as if the two of them were the only people there.

Romance.

There it was. That forbidden word. The word his family thought was silly nonsense at best and a destructive force at worst. Yet something he'd always dreamed of feeling with every cell in his body. Was that something he could safely encounter this week, too?

Not safe at all, a fact not to be forgotten. Laney was what was firing him up in the first place, making him think about things like soulmates and joy and passion. There were a list of reasons Laney could never be the woman for him. He couldn't call his grandfather to tell him the search was over.

First of all, she'd made a vow to remain single, so she wasn't even available. Second, he knew that his family expected him to partner with someone from their exclusive and privileged world. Not with a woman from Dorchester raised by a single mom. The Lusses didn't even divorce, let alone give birth out of wedlock. It had simply never happened and never would. Most importantly, most dangerously, was that he could never have a calculated and loveless agreement with her. No, around her, his blood ran hot. Boiling hot.

The only possibility with her was an impossibility. The real deal.

By the second song, Hans commended them. "That's right. Now pivot just enough for her to sense you turning her a little bit. You don't want to make her dizzy, but you can add movement."

"We're getting better," Laney said with a melting smile.

"Next," Hans addressed the room, "should you want to dance more intimately, the same rules apply. You create a frame and stay locked in it. Partners, you will feel where the leader is moving. From that, you can dance closely, you can tango, you can do any dance."

After the lesson, they decided to take the long way back to their villa. There was a dirt trail through groves of trees that provided a breezy shade from the midday sun. They exchanged hellos with another couple who crossed their path, the woman wearing a wedding veil on her wet hair, though she was in a wetsuit, as was her groom, as if they'd just engaged in a water sport. While they walked, they talked animatedly about something.

Laney smiled at the sight. "How did she keep the veil on if they went scuba diving or something like that?"

But Ian's mood had changed. A tone of cynicism flew out of his mouth. "Love conquers all."

She wasn't fazed by his sarcasm. "You really don't believe in love?"

"It's not what my family concerns itself with."

"As you've explained. You're supposed to marry for a business merger, and that's that?"

"It sounds cut and dry but it's what we've been doing for generations."

"Your parents, too?"

"Yes, I grew up in town in a house that was run like a corporation. My mother and father kept mainly separate lives. They had morning and evening check-in meetings with agendas their assistants prepared. Even spending time with my sister and me as children was scheduled."

"That sure sounds cold."

"And on Sunday afternoon, there was family time—a contrived picnic or movie date followed by dinner at my grandfather's, where he and my grandmother lived the same routine."

"Did you feel loved?"

Hmm. He'd never really thought of it like that. "I can't say I didn't. My family cares for each other. Looks out for each other. One would take a bullet for the other. I think my parents love each other, rooted in friendship and loyalty. There's just no room in our family for grand expressions and gratuitous emotions. Their position is that there's no logical purpose for romance."

"That's a strange way to grow up."

"It was. But you see, my family has only one agenda. What best serves Luss Global Holdings and protects our employees. My grandfather said it time and time again that success takes total dedication without distraction."

There was never a reason for waltzing around in the afternoon just for the heck of it. From when he was a young boy, Ian knew he was different. He observed other people, couples, and devoured dramatic books and movies. There was something that fascinated him about *feelings* even though they were frowned upon, in fact, maybe because they were frowned upon. They were what made people know they were alive, a vital nutrient. They didn't scare him or hold him back or derail him. But he had to learn to hide them. Although, as his grandfather began to push him into finding a mate, he was no longer sure he could keep everything under the lid forever.

They strolled through a particularly dense grove of low-lying plants that created a wonderful mist. It was almost like they were in another mythical world. The sun streaming in thin rays between the palm trees above made Laney's golden hair absolutely glisten. He so wanted to touch it. Run his fingers through it. Just because. On a whim. Something they might both enjoy the sensation of. If he were another person. And if they were a real couple, of course.

She mused as if she were trying to fathom him. "No one else in your family feels like they're missing out?"

His grandmother found her private way. But his sister was already carrying on the Luss tradition. She married an investment banker, and they settled outside of Boston in exclusive Weston, where they had three young children. They came into the city to have ice cream with Grandfather on Sundays. No deviation from the program.

"How well has love worked out for you?" Oh, he didn't like how that sounded coming out of his mouth. He didn't intend to lack compassion or criticize the love for Enrique that Laney spoke of, but it sounded like it ended poorly.

Nonetheless, her face fell.

"I'm sorry, that didn't come out the way I meant it."

She looked down as they continued on their path. "No. You're right. Perhaps if I hadn't fallen for someone who didn't love me back, I wouldn't be in the situation I am now. Maybe you and your family's singleness of purpose is the better way to live."

Which couldn't be less appropriate given their surroundings. The elderly couple that Ian had seen being lovey-dovey on the plane to Bermuda were ahead. They held hands and shot bright smiles to Ian and Laney as they passed by, the woman saying, "We're celebrating our sixtieth wedding anniversary."

"How lovely," Laney said enthusiastically.

"You keep falling in love with each other, as we have."

Sixty years of falling in love.

Ian wanted to cry.

CHAPTER SIX

When they got back to the villa, Ian emptied the bag of newly purchased items onto one of the big white sofas in the living room. Laney hadn't forgotten that comment he'd made about how love hadn't been working out that well for her and was still smarting a bit from it. It was true, but it really wasn't his place to say it. Fortunately, the rest of the walk through the peaceful grove and interacting with that charming elderly couple had diffused the situation.

Grabbing a pair of trunks and veering toward the small second bathroom off the living room, he said, "I'm going to change into a swimsuit, and then let's get in the water."

"Right. Sounds perfect." She took her suit into the master en suite.

She emerged a few minutes later with a tube of sunscreen. "Can you get my back?"

He cleared his throat. "Oh, yes, of course."

He seemed distant and she wondered what was on his mind. Perhaps he hadn't told a lot of people in detail about his family like he'd shared with her. Gift cards for his birthday instead of presents, regimented family togetherness times. Laney's mom had to scrimp and save to care for her daughter. Still, she always managed a little bit of spontaneity here and there, even if it was just to go out for a walk on a summer night. A life of ice cream on the third Sunday of the month from two o'clock until two thirty didn't sound healthy.

Still it was quite something that after being thrown together, Laney and Ian told each other a lot about their lives. Far beyond what she'd have figured as a maid of honor with her best man. More than she'd expect with anyone, really. Despite his fortune-focused upbringing, his family couldn't have been too terrible. He was raised to be an honorable man who had sympathy and who listened. Somehow an openness had formed between them. Like nothing she'd ever felt before.

"No one can ever get their own back, can they?" said Ian.

They walked toward each other, and she handed him the tube, then turned around.

"I wonder how people do it if they're alone." Might that be her someday?

Her vow to not put her heart on the line was unlike Ian's. For her, it was the issue of loving too much having done her in as opposed to not loving. What would being alone really be like, especially as the years rolled on? What if she was on a solo vacation and had no one to protect her middle back from harmful overexposure to the rays of the sun? Life was to be lived with others.

However, all musings were halted and siphoned out of her mind and body as soon as Ian's palm laid flat on her back. She was only human, after all, and his hand felt so lovely. She froze and was a little bit embarrassed at her automatic reaction to his touch.

"Is the cream too cold?" he asked, alarmed by her body's sudden stiffness.

"Oh, no, it's fine. Carry on." She couldn't tell him to stop.

No, she needed his ministrations. There was nothing to worry about. By the next time they did this, she'd be immune to the feel of his wide hand that pressed flat between her shoulder blades. He began swirling his hand outward in a slow spiral. That made her eyelids blink rapidly. She shouldn't let him provoke so much physical response. This was billionaire Ian Luss, who she was thrown onto this trip with by no choice of her own and who she would have no future relationship with regardless of what transpired between them. Yet, his hand on her back was intoxicating. Worse still, he seemed to be enjoying it, too, as he circled slowly over and over and over, making sure to rub in the cream, using his fingertips as needed to be sure it penetrated every inch.

A swirl with his palm, swirl with his palm, a rub in with the heel of his hand, rub in with the heel of his hand, finger in the contours, finger in the contours! The rhythm he established was completely unfair. Rendering her defenseless. Her eyes decided to fully close when his movements became overwhelming, dizzying. Fortunately, with her back to him, he didn't know that she could no longer keep her eyes open. Besides, she wanted him to finish soon. And she wanted more than anything in the world for him to not finish anytime soon.

She was sure she could feel the stream of his every exhale causing goose bumps to break out all over her skin. Was it necessary for him to stand so close that she could feel his lungs function? His hands slid down beyond the strap of her bikini top in order to apply the cream to her lower back. She made an involuntary *whoop* sound and her eyes popped open.

"Am I getting everywhere you want me to?"

Somehow those words poured out of him in a slow ooze like honey from a jar. *Am I getting everywhere you want me to?* It was an innocent question but sounded like sin with his cadence. Delectable sin that probably tasted like honey. She was glad she'd at least chosen the slightly more modest blue patterned bathing suit as opposed to the tiny triangles that comprised the black one. Still, she started imagining his hand traveling farther south than the small of her back, perhaps slipping under the fabric and squeezing and lifting and…

"Okay, I think we're good."

She inhaled and although it took all she had, she managed to take one step forward away from those hands that seemed like they were chasing her. And in fact, his hands did catch her to grab her by the sides and smooth the remaining sunscreen in his hands there.

"Wait, you don't want to burn anywhere, do you?"

She was glad that she'd put enough sunscreen on the front of her body while changing that he'd have absolutely no work there. Which isn't to say that her breasts didn't perk up at the idea of his hands getting near them. What if they had taken advantage of the beach being clothing optional and she wasn't wearing anything at all? Maybe he'd want to handle her sunscreen duties from head to toe.

Perhaps one of his hands might slip between her legs. At the thought, that very area contracted. Then released. Then contracted again. *Wow.* She ordered her body and mind to stop all of this. This had no place in the fake newlywed game.

Finally, after all of that, she turned around. He looked shocked. Blood had drained from his cheeks and his jaw was ticking. His discomfort was obvious.

"Ian, what's wrong?"

Ian wasn't doing a sufficient job at hiding his reaction after applying lucky glugs of sunscreen to Laney's supple skin. He realized the look on his face was probably a combination of unbridled arousal and utter horror. He couldn't even begin to contend with the response inside his bathing trunks. How dare she have skin like that all over! How dare her curves make a man want to keep exploring the swerves and planes until the sun went down and then rose again in the morning!

It had not occurred to him that sharing space with her was going to present this sort of a challenge. He hadn't imagined her modeling sexy bikinis in a resort shop. Or gliding around a dance floor like they were waltzing on clouds. Not to mention that he'd shared with her all sorts of personal things about himself. With a frankness he'd never spoken out loud. Her thoughts did bring him further confusion about the way his family was at odds with his soul's desire. Making him fear he might not be able to keep stuffing down his truth, which left him feeling not only exposed but like a bit of a freak.

To the matter at hand, literally, he'd have to get through this week alongside Laney's luscious flesh. Because his blood vessels told him that his reaction to her wasn't just about her alluring beauty but that she was knocking on what was buried down low. In fact, the very thing he wanted to play at here in Bermuda, like an itch he could scratch. Though he was beginning to doubt that was possible, if he'd ever be able to purge the yearning out of his system. This week could become a disaster he'd carry for life if he wasn't careful.

He lotioned himself. He'd take a chance on his back being burned sooner than he'd let her hands glide all over him the way his just had on her. He willed the inside of his trunks to settle down. The cool Atlantic would help.

"Let's go."

He threw wide the doors that opened to the balcony with its staircase leading down into the ocean. The water glistened as the sun was cresting over into late afternoon. The trade winds created a sultry breeze. Laney took the railing and descended like a Venus born of a pearl in the sea she was returning to. He quickly ran down a few stairs to get ahead of her in case she needed a hand to help her down. Husband behavior, check.

"You're so beautiful." Those words fell out of his mouth. Okay, that wasn't too much, was it? Even a woman he wouldn't be in love with but would marry might still like to hear flattery. Like flowers and chocolates, all the contrived things still had their place.

"Not if you'd heard Enrique's opinions," Laney said. "Which he had a lot of."

"About your beauty."

"About my imperfections."

"Laney, believe me, you have no imperfections."

She tilted her head in contemplation.

"What were these supposed imperfections?"

"He told me I was too lumpy."

"Aren't women supposed to be lumpy?"

"Well, my lumps weren't *elegant*—I think that was his word."

Ian's breath caught. "That's disgusting. Your lumps are everything they should be. You fell for the wrong man." No question, her lumps were quite right just as they were. Every cell in his body was in agreement with that.

"The wrong man. I thought you didn't believe in the *meant to be* mate."

"Not for me. I have hopes for you." He chuckled.

"No way."

With that, they stepped off the last stair and into the ocean, which at that point was only ankle deep. They proceeded to walk farther and farther straight into the water as if they were promenading down the wedding aisle to be married. He wanted to take her arm in his, but of course, didn't, as a weird underwater wedding ceremony was probably the last thing on her mind.

When the water reached their waists, they

both dove in, immersing themselves in the cool, clear water. After a few swim strokes, they bobbed their heads up. The water brushed back all of Laney's hair, leaving her shining face exposed, so exquisite it stole Ian's breath.

By the end of the day, Laney and Ian were tired. They decided to make do with the many gourmet snacks and big bowl of fresh fruit that had been left for them in the villa and to call for a proper dinner the next day. A countertop held raised platters with a variety of nuts, cheeses, salads, breads and the gooiest chocolate brownies ever made. There was more than enough to munch on, and they washed it all down with refreshing fruit drinks. Neither cared to open the champagne on ice.

They sat outside on lounge chairs facing the ocean's horizon as the sun set, watching the sky turn almost every color of the rainbow from red to orange to pink to the dark of night. They spoke of trivial matters, childhood things that weren't heavy like they had before—about Laney's poverty and lack of a father and Ian's family with their strange customs. They counted the stars in the sky.

When they decided to go inside, there *it* was, just as they'd left it before they went out. The master bedroom. Still easy to locate by the trail of rose petals that remained on the rich wooden floorboards. And the bed decorated with the gigantic rose petal heart. Where couples immersed in passion, the enticing scent of the flowers reminding them with every breath that tonight was one of the most significant nights of their lives.

Laney thought she might have had a honeymoon night like this with the man she thought loved her. A night to remember with every tiny detail as special as it could be. One she'd treasure not only through photos and videos but in her soul and heart as a commemoration of the beginning of the rest of their lives.

Instead, she was acting in this strange and almost tragic play, one that to Ian was emancipating. Whereas he was clearly fantasizing about a romantic love he wouldn't have, it could turn painful for her if she let herself get sucked into any of it. She was here to recreate, and there was nothing wrong with doing so in the company of a soulful man as long as she kept reality front and center in her mind.

Ian said it first. "We haven't discussed the sleeping arrangements."

Right. Exactly.

"It's kind of funny, all of this elaborate honeymoon stuff just for us. No one knowing that we're just bunking together."

"I'll have to remember to definitely *not* book a place like this for my own honeymoon when the time comes."

"What do you mean?"

He leaned over to the bed to run his hand through the velvety rose petals. "This. Champagne and petals. The romance checklist."

"You don't even want that on your honeymoon?"

"I suppose if my bride wanted it. As long as she understood that it's just for show. That our purpose is to produce the heir and the spare."

"Do you have that etched on a plaque in the office conference room?"

His face shot sharply toward hers, and for a moment, she was worried she had insulted him. His family was clearly suffocating, but she had no right to pass judgment on it.

"I do know one thing," he said after whatever bothered him had passed. "One of us could surely sleep on a sofa or one of the loungers on the balcony."

Sleeping outside alone. That didn't sound too good. "What if creatures from the sea with gigantic tentacles swept up to the mainland, encircled me and pulled me into the ocean? I wouldn't want that to be your fate, either."

"Glad to hear, thank you."

She glanced into the living room at the two sofas as if they would have gone anywhere since she last looked at them. And then she eyed the ginormous bed again.

"That's not a standard size, is it? It has to be custom-made. It's so big." There was fear in her voice.

Surely she wasn't worried that Ian was going to morph into one of those woman-eating invertebrates with tentacles and capture her, turning her into a sea creature who existed only for his pleasure.

Oh, Lordy. What was she thinking, and why did that sound not half bad? A crazy little wave splashed through her insides. Him capturing her with his tentacles.

"Yes, that bed looks as if it were custom-made." His jaw jutted forward. He was having some thoughts of his own.

"I'd imagine we can put a row of pillows down the center as a barrier and do okay."

"A barrier to what?" His eyebrows rose.

"I just… I just…maybe seems a little inappropriate to be sharing a bed with…"

"Don't worry, I think I'll be able to make it through the evening without throwing myself on you." It might not have been him that she was worried about. Reminiscing about his hand thoroughly rubbing that sunscreen into her back was enough to make her grow a couple of tentacles herself.

"I'm sorry, I didn't mean to imply anything. It's only—well, come on, this is unusual, isn't it?"

He turned his head away from her, but she followed it until she could get him to look into her eyes again. She hadn't meant to accuse him of anything untoward. And she was probably silly to think for even a minute that he might have been contemplating the activities that could transpire in that bed meant for lovers. He certainly wasn't thinking of said activities with *her*. Even though he professed to like her lumps, they both knew what he was after in a woman. And what she wasn't.

Although he was hard to second-guess. His eyes were so mesmerizing, dark and big. Like someone could just jump into them and be immersed, whole and surrounded. They locked stares for far too long. With all the strength she had, she was the one to finally pull away.

His face twitched a little bit. She didn't dare imagine it was disappointment.

Finally, he said, "I do tend to toss around in my sleep, so let's use many pillows for your barricade."

He gestured at the dozen or so along the headboard. Turquoise, silver and blue cases covered pillows of varying sizes. Together, they built a sort of fortress going down a straight line from top to bottom, quite evenly dividing the bed in half, scattering some of the rose petals in the process. They backed off at the foot and checked their handiwork.

"This is like summer camp," she remarked.

"I didn't go to summer camp."

"Neither did I." She shrugged.

"In any case, it'll do."

He dug into his bag for a T-shirt, and headed over to the extra bathroom. While he was away, she slipped into the master bath to wash up and change as well. A peach-colored tank top with matching pajama shorts was what she'd brought to sleep in after the wedding. She claimed one side of the bed as hers and brought a bottle of water, a tablet and a book to the nightstand. She couldn't think of anything else she'd need for the night.

It was no big deal, she told herself. She was

just going to spend the night—oh, wait, the week—with Ian, sharing the same bed. Once they stepped out the villa doors, they were Mr. and Mrs. Luss, but in here, they were just acquaintances taking advantage of an unused ritzy vacation.

It's no big deal, she chanted to herself. They should be able to just kick back and relax. No big deal. Her heart was beating faster than normal, but it was no big deal…

She climbed into bed and watched Ian re-enter the room. He tucked himself into his side, and when both of them were lying on their backs, they couldn't see each other over the pillow wall they'd built.

"Goodnight then," he said, somewhat abruptly.

"The fragrance of these rose petals is really strong."

"G'night." He was done talking.

Hours later, she was still awake, willing morning to come. She listened to Ian breathing in rhythmic slumber. A thought circled around her, indeed like a tentacled beast, except this one was yelling at her to hold on and brace herself. Because the tide was rising.

CHAPTER SEVEN

IAN WONDERED WHAT a honeymoon night for a regular couple was supposed to be like as he tried not to toss and turn too much in the bed. He supposed it would surround the betrothed in a celestial cocoon. Whether it was filled with tender affection or driving passion, it would be the couple's own. It was a snapshot of their marriage they'd hold forever. He guessed that's what it would have been like if Melissa and Clayton were in this bed as intended. They'd have already had a wedding night in the presidential suite of the Fletcher Club, probably been excited and elated and punch-drunk from the wedding and reception. Plus, they already lived together, so it wasn't like in older times when the wedding night was the first time they'd have sex.

By tonight, here at the villa, they would have been able to finally exhale into the hope and calm that they believed matrimony was to bring them. Ian figured that even sick and gray in Boston from the food poisoning, they were managing moments of both positive memories and plans for the future. He was sure their good humor would incorporate the offending oysters into their personal folklore.

As for Ian, he was as restless as a slippery eel. He couldn't see over the pillow wall to gauge whether or not Laney was sleeping. The bed was so big that her movements didn't even register on his side. All he knew was that he was sleepy but wide awake at the same time, and this was turning into a nightmare of a honeymoon night.

He was ruminating over and over again on two points. One was what a genuine night on a honeymoon would be like for him. The other was on the pretend bride he found himself in bed with. He couldn't get off the idea that a lot of realness had actually passed between them and that, in her company, he experienced himself in a way he never had before. Which was absurd, because in reality, it was just the situation that was getting to him.

Still, that authenticity with her nagged at him. It was so unexpected. He thought about that creep Enrique making her feel unwanted and how he'd like to give him a piece of his mind. Not treating her right in the first place and then leaving when her café burned down. Unconscionable. Not that there was anything to be done about it.

He tried to clear his head and meditate until the morning finally broke.

He finally heard Laney's voice after he'd watched the slow turn of sunrise over the ocean through the master bedroom windows. Feeling it was okay to do so, he yanked a few of the pillows separating them and tossed them to the floor.

"How did you sleep?" Laney asked.

"Great," he lied. "How about you?"

She rolled over onto her side toward him, and he followed suit to face her, but he was careful not to get too close physically. "Slept like a baby."

"Where does that expression come from? Babies wake up all night screaming for bottles or to be held, don't they?"

"Yeah, I guess so. How about I slept like a rock?"

"That makes more sense." Now he was engaging in pillow talk while Laney's hair splayed across the sheets, absolutely shimmering in the glow of morning. It was like every moment shared with her was a special one. As if he wasn't waking to the world alone. Just like a couple in love.

He needed to put a stop to all of those thoughts. It was one thing to go through all the actions and even feelings a newly married man might have. But it was another entirely to start thinking of Laney as his real wife. He needed to figure out a way to balance immersing himself in the encounter while not forgetting what it wasn't. That would have to be enough. They should get out of bed immediately. As a matter of fact, out of the villa.

"Shall we get some breakfast? Let's go to one of the restaurants."

"Good morning, and congratulations." The restaurant hostess identified them as honeymooners as soon as Ian mentioned which villa they were in.

With him in a pair of khakis and an untucked white shirt plus a pair of sneakers and Laney in a pretty white dress with orange-and-green-flower detail that she must have brought to wear to one of the wedding events, they appeared as a newly married couple enjoying the paradise they were surrounded by. The outdoor restaurant was under a canopy of shade plants. Every table set a bit apart from the next, with foliage hedges to make each one private.

"Look around," Laney half whispered, "there are only tables for two."

"Yes, remember, this is a couples-only resort."

"What if we made friends while we were here?"

"Let's don't. We already have enough to do convincing the staff that we're a couple."

A waiter arrived with two odd white mugs filled with coffee. Each was shaped into a curvy heart. Ian wasn't exactly sure where he was supposed to sip from, so he took an awkward slurp.

The waiter asked, "Lovers' breakfast for two?"

Ian didn't have a clue as to what lovers ate for breakfast that was different than what ordinary mortals did, but he wanted to find out.

"Well, that's a…presentation." Laney chose her words carefully when the meal was served.

A carafe of mimosas was brought to the table in an ice bucket shaped and painted like a top hat. The waiter poured the drink into two champagne flutes, which were made of glass but also curiously heart-shaped.

Once he left Laney asked, "How do they

manufacture mugs and champagne glasses shaped into hearts?"

"I've never seen them before. I'd guess it's just a question of making the molds."

All the tables that Ian could see had the same setup. A couple of women laughed heartily. A young couple sat in silence. Perhaps something had gone wrong the night before in the lovemaking department. Or there had been an argument about something petty. A couples' resort could be fraught with potential peril, there was so much expecatation. Once again, keeping emotions out of partnering made so much sense. The right woman for Ian would be the one who didn't make him feel.

Ian wouldn't put his Luss wife, when he found her, through having to deal with things like heart-shaped mugs and big smiles if she didn't want them. That was a relief.

Laney brought her mug close to his. "See, they fit together."

She slid the open curve side of her mug into the rounded side of his until they formed a whole. Like the yin and yang symbol. Representing togetherness. One bending to accommodate the other. In flow, in fullness.

As she locked her mug into place, her finger ran along his, which gave his body another one of those tingles. This was the spell lovers cast over each other. A mere touch could change the other's physiology. He was sure that if he and Laney had a legitimate honeymoon night, nothing would have gone wrong in their lovemaking. In fact, he would have seen to it that what transpired in their bed would have been something to remember for the rest of their lives.

Next, a tray was brought to the table. On top of it was a dome formed of white lace.

"It's a wedding veil!" Laney exclaimed, showing Ian the way the fabric gathered to a point that was attached to a clear plastic comb. "See, that's what goes in your hair."

"My hair?"

She laughed. "It could. Traditionally, it would be for my hair. You know, Melissa wore one."

"Yes, I know what a wedding veil is, I just don't know why it's on top of my eggs."

"Romance." They both sniggered.

"Well, thank you for clearing that up. I had no idea how unromantic my breakfasts had been in the past."

They dug into their eggs, breakfast meats and the basket of hot toast.

"Yes, the toast is heart-shaped," Laney said.

"Couldn't they think of some other shape to make the toast?"

"Like what?"

"What about round with a little protruding triangle like a diamond ring?"

"I love it! I'm going to suggest that to the chef."

"No, let's keep it a secret, and you can use it for your café when you open one."

Laney's head dropped sideways, looking both at him and past him. "You're so sure I'm going to?"

"Well, of course. Why not?"

"Nothing. I just appreciate the vote of confidence."

"Right. What that idiot you were with didn't give you."

She studied him in a silence that said more than a thousand words could. This funny, smart, lovely woman had not been valued. In a parallel world, he might like to spend the rest of his life showing Laney just how wonderful and appreciated she was.

"We should go before they give us a cake shaped like a wedding dress," she joked with a childlike enthusiasm.

"Do you think they might?"

As they strolled back to the villa, an idea hit Ian. "Unless you had something in mind for today, I'd like to take you somewhere."

"Okay."

He punched numbers into his phone.

Seemingly minutes after his call, he heard a car pull up alongside the villa. Adalson from the staff exited the high-end sports car convertible as Ian opened the front door. "For your leisure, Mr. Luss."

Laney, apparently hearing that they had a visitor, came to the door as well.

"How are you this morning, Mrs. Luss?"

"Great, thanks."

They were becoming less and less shocked every time they heard themselves referred to as husband and wife. In fact, it was becoming natural. That was the plan. Ian continued the conversation with himself as they sped up the highway. He wanted all of these married couple situations. For example, it would be okay if he thought his wife was pretty and intelligent and interesting, wouldn't it? As long as he didn't fall in love with her. Okay, that was tricky. In the meantime, Laney would have achieved her goal of relaxing and gearing up to start again in Boston. Then they would go their separate ways.

Of course, as much as he told himself all of that, his mind was a confused jumble, and his heart was sending messages that were becoming impossible to ignore.

"Where are we going?" Laney asked as Ian took the turns of the highway, wind blowing their hair.

"We'll be there in a few minutes," he answered and reached across the car's center console to squeeze to her forearm.

He didn't mean to do that. Which made him again question attraction and desire and how he was going to keep that all straight. Because the minute his fingers made contact with Laney's lithe arm, he wanted to leave it there and cursed the road for needing both of his hands on the steering wheel to navigate the twists as he steered inland from the coastal highway. They reached the saltwater pond surrounded by marshland that he'd read about.

"I thought it might be nice to be in still water today before we go back into the ocean."

As can only happen when one is staying at a top-notch resort where the answer is never *no*, the rowboat he requested was at shore. Alongside it were blankets and a basket no doubt filled with goodies.

"We're rowing?"

"I'm rowing. Your job is to take in the atmosphere." A charge ran through him at his own words. He was about to embark on something scary to him. And it wasn't using oars.

He helped her into the boat, where she sat on one of the two benches. With feet still on dry ground, he pushed the boat into the water and then quickly climbed in. He sat on the opposite bench facing her. He took the oars and began rowing away from shore.

It was happening. They were in a rowboat, the only ones in the pond. The sky was blue. There was enough breeze in the air to keep it from being hot. The overgrowth of the marshes swayed gently. He was reenacting a scene from a movie he remembered first seeing when he was a young teen, just at puberty.

In the movie he'd since watched many times, an impossibly handsome strapping man in a white shirt with the sleeves rolled up was rowing a boat like this. Across from him sat a beautiful redheaded woman with pale skin and freckles. She wore a wide-brimmed straw hat with a black ribbon. All of which made them appear like they were in a period piece, although, actually, it was present day when the film was made.

The sort of classicism of the way the couple looked made an impression on young hormonal Ian. Like a painting come to life. The woman was ethereal in her beauty and pure in her grace. As the man rowed, he was solely responsible for her safety, and reveling in that honor and responsibility, their eyes told each other how in love they were.

Ian was so moved by the gesture of manhood in his rowing, something he'd never felt so distinctly before. It wasn't a question of the woman being dependent or fragile. It was simply that in taking charge of the rowboat, he was able to directly display his own masculinity and chivalry in a way that felt so natural, not confusing like the rest of puberty was.

Someday, he told himself back then, someday he would take a woman rowing, and she'd smile a pretty smile, and the thing that passed between couples would pass between them, giving him stature, giving him pride, giving him his place.

Of course, that was all before he understood about family codes and the Luss way of doing things. Secretly, though, he always hoped he'd get a once-in-a-lifetime chance to live out that scene from the movie that meant so much to him.

With his pulse jumping, lower parts in total chaos and all of his will, he embarked on the next part of the scene, when the man stands up in the boat and sings to his beloved. When he was teen, Ian had rehearsed it in front of the mirror using a variety of popular love songs. This time, he was going to sing the song that he and Laney had danced disastrously to at the wedding: "Meant as a Pair." That was going to be *their* song.

He took a wide stance to balance himself in the boat. "What I want is right there. We were meant as a pair. I would walk without fear," he crooned at the top of his lungs, a smiling Laney looking up at him with sparkling eyes. "Every moment we share."

Almost in disbelief that this moment was finally coming true, Ian stretched his arms out as wide as they would open, feeling the freest he'd ever been…

And with that the rowboat toppled over, submerging him and Laney down into the pond.

Oh, cripes! That wasn't part of the scene. He quickly brought his head above water and saw Laney's bobbing as well. "Are you okay?"

"Yes," she called out.

He swam the few strokes to her. The water wasn't deep, and they were able to get their footing. Holding her, he brushed her now wet and weedy hair back from her face.

"I'm so sorry."

"I'll bet," she said with a grin.

Without remembering not to, or deciding to ignore remembering not to, he took her face in his hands and brought his lips to hers. At first, he just brushed his against hers, taking in their pillowy coolness. But the second— yes, second—kiss lasted longer.

Ian didn't pull away. Didn't want to. He pressed his lips into hers with urgency. Which she met. And then he did it again. And again. The more he kissed her, the more he wanted to. His hands caressed her cheeks, finding her bones, getting to know them with his fingers while his lips still pressed into her plush mouth.

His lips parted so that his tongue could meet hers. Warm, almost hot, his throat let out a little moan he couldn't prevent. His hands moved to the back of her head so that he could bring her closer. Her hair was soaked and heavy. His mouth roamed from her forehead to her nose to her chin to her jaw.

This wasn't how the scene ended in that movie from his childhood. It simply cut to the next where the couple continued to flirt. The reenacting was over. This was real life.

Laney picked some leaves from his hair.

"Do you know anything about the Bermuda Triangle?" he asked in between kisses after it popped into his mind. "Why does this place have that name and reputation?"

"I read about it on the plane. It's also called the Devil's Triangle. A geographical region of the Atlantic Ocean where strange disappearances have supposedly taken place."

Disappear with me, Laney.

He kissed her again. "Strange how?"

"People say there's some kind of supernatural vortex."

"What has disappeared?"

"Supposedly, aircraft and ships, although there's no scientific proof. Mostly around the mid-twentieth century. There was a famous case of five navy torpedo bombers that went missing. But when the investigations were complete, they had just run out of fuel."

He kissed her yet again. Maybe there *was* something supernatural about Bermuda. He was definitely being absorbed into a vortex. The Laney Triangle.

Lifeguard! Rescue ship! SOS! Someone please pull Laney away from Ian's insistent lips! Talk about the Bermuda Triangle.

She had those thoughts, yet it was like a dream in which somebody was mouthing words but no sounds were coming out. Maybe because her mouth was completely preoccupied. Her hair was sopping wet, she was mucky, her clothed body still immersed in water, yet none of that mattered. Not when Ian's seductive lips mashed against her mouth, hungry and demanding. She'd never been kissed like this and knew immediately that every kiss she'd receive for the rest of her life, if there were any, would be dull in comparison.

He tilted his head one way and then the other as he took from her with his mouth. In return, he tasted like the sweet and tart lemonade they had sipped in the boat before it capsized. Nothing had ever tasted so good. His kisses were telling her something. A mystery about him. Or a piece of wisdom about what two people could share. For someone who professed to have no future that included romance, his lips told another story. One of passion. One of bond. One of naked truth.

"What are you doing to me, Laney?" he whispered against her mouth, unwilling to pull himself away to even ask the question. The vibration of his lips as he spoke each word confirmed she was in the earthly world and not hallucinating. "I can't get enough of kissing you."

"This isn't supposed to be happening." There. As if saying that out loud excused the predicament. Yet they kept kissing. "There's no one around. We don't have to pretend to be a couple."

"I don't know what's come over me."

"We should stop."

They should have. They didn't. She wrapped her arms around his neck, feeling the wetness of his shirt collar under his hair.

"Laney."

Ian's loveless mission made no sense. Enrique's rejection of her—and he never kissed her like that anyway—made no sense. The only thing that made sense was Ian and Laney in the middle of a mucky pond in the middle of an island in the middle of an ocean. That was all there was and all that mattered.

Wait a minute! "Ian, stop. Stop."

He respected her sudden exclamation and pulled back.

"We can't do this. We're not together. Nor will we ever be."

He raked his fingers back through his long hair that, while wet, almost brushed his shoulders. Impossibly sexy. "Of course, you're right. It must have been those stupid heart-shaped mugs at breakfast that made my mental circuits cross-fire. Or your devastatingly beautiful face."

"It's weird when you call me beautiful." Weird and sort of painful, like a wound re-opening.

"But you are."

She smiled with a nod, "Enrique wanted me to have cosmetic surgery on my nose."

Ian stretched out his middle finger, which he used to stroke from the top of her nose all the way down to where it met her lips. "What on earth is wrong with your nose?"

"He thought it would look better if it tipped up at the end."

Ian gritted his teeth in disapproval. "That's repulsive, don't you think? I mean, I don't begrudge someone wanting to correct something they don't like about their appearance. But to have that come from someone else? That's just sick."

"Thank you for saying that, Ian," she sighed with a slow exhale. "I didn't think I would ever get close to a man after everything with him. But spending this time with you is making me realize that maybe I could someday, far in the future. With a better man. When everything doesn't conjure up bad memories anymore."

"If you were mine… I'm sure you'll meet the right person someday."

If you were mine.

He stopped himself after that, knowing she could never be his, and it seemed like he sensed it was best not to finish his thought and have it in the atmosphere. She, too, knew that outcome wasn't possible so there had to be a limit on how far this fantasy enactment that they were together went.

"What about you? Ian, those kisses just then didn't feel like they came from a man who has no interest in passion."

"It's your fault. You bring it out in me."

"My fault? Nah, you don't get to tag me with that one," she said with a nervous giggle.

"The secluded pond, your pretty dress, the rowboat, the song. I…lost my reserve."

"Probably something that doesn't happen to you much."

"Never again, if I can help it. You're dangerous, miss."

They smiled at each other for a bit too long. Okay, a lot too long. She had a responsibility here. He could potentially become out of control with this pretend honeymoon, and for her own safety, she needed to make sure that didn't happen. His effusive compliments. That passion directed at her. He was living out the person he truly was inside, maybe for the first and last time. It was like a dream. Too much to ask for her to play along without forgetting the temporary nature of it all.

She was only human, and being treated so nicely was something she was unfortunately not accustomed to. She wasn't immune to romance, either. It was all on her to keep it from going too far, as much fun as it was. To remember that she was on a magical adventure where the sand was pink, the man kissed like his life depended on it, and in a week's time, she'd be in Boston looking for a job and a place to live. Ian would return to buying mountain ranges, and they'd have some unforgettable memories to file away in a locked mental shoebox.

"We should get out of the water."

When they returned to the villa, after they finished picking marsh weeds from each other's hair and clothes, they retreated to separate showers.

His cheeks were flushed as he entered the bedroom afterward, dressed in a thick white robe and drying his hair with a towel. He regarded the bed, which had been cleaned and made up by the resort staff. Tonight's extra touch after the cascade of rose petals from the night before was a single chocolate rose and a scattering of individually wrapped other chocolates on the pillows.

Laney brushed the chocolates into her hand and put them on the nightstand. "We'll have to rebuild our pillow fort. I wonder what the housekeeper thought."

"On second thought, why don't I just grab a few pillows, and I'll sleep on one of the sofas," he said and gestured into the living room.

"Oh." She felt a sting of rejection. "Okay. Or I could."

"No, no, I insist. You enjoy the bed."

She didn't want to ask the reason for his decision. Although she knew fully well what it was. After those kisses that shouldn't have happened, he didn't want to share a bed with her. She could understand. The attraction to each other at the pond was not diminished now that they were back at the resort. Quite the opposite.

The villa was Mr. and Mrs. Luss's home away from home and felt as such. It was only too easy to imagine the next logical course of action. After a day together that included a lengthy interlude of kissing, they would fall into bed to continue. In fact, it might take making love all night long to satisfy the fervor for each other that had built up under the warm sunny skies. It was hard to even think of anything else.

She managed to say, "I'll order dinner."

CHAPTER EIGHT

WHEN SUNLIGHT STREAMED into the villa's living room, Ian was glad he was lying on his back on the sofa. He looked up to the whirl of the ceiling fan that had kept him cool all night. And cooling off was what he had needed following the events of yesterday. He was supposed to be practicing so that he'd have advanced knowledge of how to behave when he met the woman he was to marry. Husband training. The island, the resort, eggs under a wedding veil.

If only he'd stopped there. He'd had that adolescent memory of the movie where the man was rowing a boat with a pretty redhead on a tranquil pond. And he got to live that out. It really did fill his heart to indulge in the romantic notions he'd thought so much about. Even if he had to leave it at that, at just the once. Then, like an idiot, he accidentally tipped the boat over, which led to wet hair and a whole bunch of kisses. A whole bunch. An amount and quality he would not easily forget.

So the lesson learned was that he should not marry someone he wanted to kiss that much.

"Good morning." Laney made her way into the living room from the master suite, rubbing her eyes to get the sleep dust out of them. "I'm hungry. Are we ready for eggs under the wedding veil again?"

"I was reading that a Bermuda breakfast is a *thing*. Let's skip the bridal brekkie ball and go into town. I found a place that's well rated for serving an authentic Sunday codfish breakfast."

"It's not Sunday."

"That's what it's called, and the restaurant prefers to make money every day."

"Ha ha. Okay, I'll throw some clothes on."

She retreated to get dressed.

He tried to shut down the vision, but failed, that she'd be removing clothes in order to put others on.

As they tooled off the resort grounds in the sports car that now had become theirs for use, Laney adjusted herself in the car seat. She'd put on a white blouse that had a little ruffling at the V neckline, a tan skirt and a pair of beige sandals, all of which she'd picked up at the resort shops. He glanced over to her bare legs. She caught him doing so and adjusted her skirt again. He sensed she was feeling awkward about the kiss fest. He wasn't sure whether there was anything left to discuss about it, though. They'd agreed quite matter-of-factly on the drive back that it was a mistake and wouldn't happen again.

His body had told him otherwise in the shower when they'd returned to the villa. While she went to the en suite rainforest shower that had become hers, he again took the smaller bathroom. It was a more than adequate shower, and once in, he soaped up to wash off the pond water that had saturated through his clothes. Using the thick bar of sea-breeze-scented soap directly against his tight skin, he circled everywhere, hoping the suds would relax all of the tension that had built by his and Laney's torrent of kisses.

Unfortunately, all the ocean fragrance and running water served to do was arouse him further, making his groin surge for relief. He pulsed at the thought of her soaping herself up in the other shower. Then he indulged in an even more dangerous thought. If he was the one lathering her. Wasn't he supposed to be picturing elephants in the shower to keep those thoughts at bay? It wasn't working.

Then he was throbbing and turned the shower faucet to a cooler temperature in hopes that would calm his inflamed body. Yet, all he could concentrate on was running his palms down her arms in the pond, skimming along the swell of her breasts, noting in that instant how firm yet pliable they were. As the water cascaded down on him, he succumbed to a mental replay of the swirl of their tongues. He stroked his erection. At first, slowly, like the kisses. Until his whole body began to rollick and he became desperate for release. With long pulls he massaged into his need, bringing himself powerfully closer, closer, closer and then finally into an explosion that left him shaking under the water tap until his heart rate returned to normal. Once he recovered, he toweled off.

"There it is." When they got into the capital city of Hamilton, Ian pointed to the homey-looking shack.

Now that he'd spent most of the car ride reliving his urgent needs from last night, he implored himself to at least be present and enjoy breakfast with Laney, who should *not* be in his shower in any form and with whom he would *not* engage in any further activity that would make it appear otherwise. What he could do was quell his ravenous hunger with a huge breakfast.

He'd found the restaurant online, and they chose a table under the shade awning. About half of the tables were taken.

A tall slim man in a floral printed shirt greeted them. "Welcome. You ready for a big greeze?"

"We're tourists, what does that mean?" Laney asked.

"A great big meal. You're gonna let this old onion feed you a Bermy breakfast?"

"Yes, thanks. Onion?"

"Born and bred. We get that nickname because Bermuda onions are known all over the world. Call me Dack."

"Yes, feed us, please."

"You're staying at Pink Shores."

"How could you tell?"

"The glow of love. You can spot it a mile away."

Although what had passed between Ian and Laney was *not* love, he liked that it showed.

Dack quickly brought glasses of icy water, and they both took sips. "The codfish breakfast, right?"

"Yeah, we're here to try it."

As their food was being prepared, Ian asked, "So tell me about this café you want to open. Why a café in the first place?"

"I like café culture. I like to read and look out a window and sip something warm in the winter and cold in the summer. Of course, coffee and tea cost more than they used to, but you don't have to be a millionaire to buy a place to sit and unwind and daydream for an hour."

"Did you go to a lot of cafés when you were younger?"

"Oh yeah. There weren't many in Dorchester, but when I was a teenager, on the weekend, I'd take the T and find them all over the city."

"Because you liked looking out the window with a cup of coffee?"

"My mom worked all the time. So sure, it was nice to be around other people and just hang out. I didn't really like school."

A teenager with a working mom and a dad who'd skipped out. What lousy examples of men she'd had in her life. That knotted in Ian's gut. His family took care of their own.

"With all the brand-name coffee houses, is running your own café a viable business?"

He couldn't help but put his professional hat on. Maybe he could help her.

"Well, I doubt anyone is going to get rich that way, but my business plan shows me making a living for myself after the first year when the expenses of opening are paid off."

"The codfish breakfast." Dack returned, each hand holding both an enormous plate and a smaller one. Once he laid everything down, he said, "Eat well."

"Oh my," Laney said as she surveyed what looked like enough food for a party. "What do we have here?"

"That's salted codfish." Dack pointed to the piles of shredded white fish. "Then boiled potatoes. Boiled eggs. Bananas. Avocado. Those are the traditional foods."

She gestured to the smaller plate that contained pancakes. "Corn cakes?"

"We call them johnny cakes. All right now, you dig in."

Ian forked up one of the potato slices and piled a bit of the codfish on top. The salt of the fish was nicely cut by the bland potato.

"Oh, I like the banana with the fish." Laney chimed in as they tried various combinations from their plate. "Such simple foods but so delicious together."

"I want to hear more about the café." Ian loved that Laney had something so well thought out that she wanted for herself and that even though the Pittsfield place burned down, she was planning to start again.

"I'd like it to have a cozy feel. A small library on bookshelves where people could either donate a book or take one they wanted to read. Big comfortable furniture. Although, of course, all new and gleaming equipment behind the counter."

"That sounds like Café Emilia in New York. Have you ever been there?"

"No. That's the most famous Greenwich Village café. It's been there for, what, a hundred years?"

"You have to see it. It sounds like what you have in mind."

"I'm not glad Melissa and Clayton got sick, but I have to admit, it's nice being on this unexpected trip. It's getting my mind going about the future."

Ian was worried that his mind was going in a direction he couldn't let it. He dug into his food again.

While they were taking a walk afterward, his phone buzzed. The sound of crashing waves made it a challenge to hear.

"Grandfather, I'm at the beach."

"That's all right, Ian, I won't keep you. I'm just calling to let you know that I have the contact information for some women I'd like you to have dinner with."

Ian looked over at Laney beside him as they strolled barefoot in the sand, shoes in hand, the wind tousling her hair, a fun retro-type pair of sunglasses on her face. He didn't want to meet the women his grandfather had selected.

No one was going to compare to the woman he was with. The lines between practicing at being a husband and real feelings for Laney had become thoroughly blurred.

After exploring Hamilton, they toured the Crystal Cave and its magnificent mineral formations, thousands of powdery stalactites growing downward from the roof. Then it was back into the convertible, and Ian drove them toward the villa.

"If we can ever eat again after that breakfast, we have a booking for dinner at the resort's formal dining room," Ian said.

"Oh. I didn't notice that on the reservations. Melissa and Clayton booked it?" Laney asked.

"If you'd like to go, that is. Otherwise, I can cancel it."

"What would we do instead?" Laney turned her head toward Ian, whose eyes faced forward on the road ahead.

"Huh" escaped his lips.

What would we do instead? She was crazy to ask that aloud.

Surely what they should not do is be alone together. Not when memories of his kisses played over and over again on the sense memory of her skin. When her soul ached for more and her body tingled at the thought.

And if all of that wasn't bad enough, he had to go and say supportive things about her aspirations. As if her goal wasn't totally *basic*, as Enrique had criticized when he begrudgingly bought the café in Pittsfield. Ian heard her ideas as valid and interesting.

"Well, I've got a problem," she said.

"I'll try to have a solution."

That's how he thought. In solutions. She loved that about him. *Oops.* She *liked* that about him. She would never have any reason to *love* anything about Ian Luss. Enrique had all the right answers in the beginning, and look how that turned out.

"I don't have anything to wear. Everything I have with me is too casual," said Laney.

"I have a couple of suits with me, so I'm

set. Book a personal shopper at the formal wear boutique at the resort. We'll buy you something as soon as we get back."

Again, Ian Luss was living on another planet than she was. Just book a shopper, buy a dress—that seemed obvious to him.

"If we've used up the shopping allowance, I'm paying for it, so there's no discussion about that."

Another matter of fact for him. Money, or lack thereof, was never an obstacle. Her life had been totally different on that score. Always budgeting, always compromising. Adding to the surrealness of this week were sports cars and rowboats and now, apparently, clothes.

When they got back to the central compound of the resort, Hans was leading one of his ballroom dancing lessons. Since they were trying to get to the shop, they didn't have time for a full lesson, but Ian waltzed Laney across the atrium to get to the other end.

"Well done," Hans yelled out to them. "You have the basics."

Laney was pleased by his comment.

They exchanged hellos with the older couple who had wished them the same sixty years of happiness they had shared. Laney adored how they took turns sipping from a paper cup of coffee while sitting on a bench by the fountain.

"Mr. and Mrs. Luss, I'm Solene." The austere, stiff-backed personal shopper introduced herself when they arrived at the dress shop.

Mannequins here and there were draped in high-fashion clothes, from a beaded gown to a little black dress worn with a strand of pearls to an architectural dress sculpted with a diagonal sash of fabric flowers. Laney was sure they'd be able to find something suitable for the evening.

Ian explained that they were dining in the formal room.

Solene asked, "What type of dress do you prefer?"

Laney didn't know. She thought of a time she had gotten dressed for a family function of Enrique's, and he didn't like what she was wearing. She understood *change into something else* in an entirely new way that night. That was the night she realized she'd never be who he wanted her to be. In fact, if she was honest with herself, that was the night she knew he would leave her. Her biggest regret was that she didn't leave him first.

She blurted, "Something simple."

"You looked great in green at the wedding," Ian explained to Solene, "She was the maid of honor."

Oops.

"At the wedding of some friends of ours last month," Laney said, jumping in, covering for Ian's foible.

He bit his lip in the most adorable way, like a five-year-old with his hand caught in the cookie jar.

"I like blue, too."

"I think you'd look best in a belted dress with a full skirt," Solene suggested. "That would flatter your figure."

Why did she make *flatter* sound like an insult? Thank heavens Laney had been able to shop on her own for those swimsuits in the casual shop the other day. Otherwise, the saleswomen there would have had a field day!

Ian must have seen the reaction in her face, because he chimed in. "Solene, you don't have to worry about that. Laney looks fantastic in everything."

A grin broke out on Laney's face that she couldn't contain. He was a special man, even if his future entailed squelching the best of himself. The pride and old-fashioned charm he had while rowing them on that boat, serenading her—wow. Before the tip-over, of course.

"Would you like to follow me to the dressing room?" Solene asked.

Laney couldn't lie. The shimmery navy-colored dress with a belt made of the same fabric did look great on her. The scooped neckline revealed plenty of cleavage but remained utterly tasteful. The full skirt wasn't too much, and it fell to midcalf. Laney thought that was called tea length.

"I like it."

"Would you like to show your husband?"

Husband lingered in the air for a few seconds, sounding like far too lovely a word. As for the dress, she knew she didn't need his approval, but she wanted it nonetheless. So she nodded and came out from the dressing room.

He raised his eyebrows at her. "My wife, you look stunning as usual."

"You like it, husband?"

"I do."

"*I do.* You've been saying those two words a lot lately, haven't you?"

"They will never get old."

Solene ducked into a storage area and reappeared with boxes. She opened them and removed two pairs of shoes. One pair were the highest, thinnest, heels Laney had ever seen, the vamp crusted in jewels that would go with the color of the dress. The second pair also had sky-high heels and a bunch of ribbons she didn't understand.

"Do you have any flats?" It was her honeymoon, after all. She deserved to be comfortable.

"Of course. But I think you'll find that a high heel gives a long and lean look that won't be achieved with flats."

There we go again. There was always something not perfect about her. She wasn't *long* enough. She wasn't *lean* enough.

"Let's see." Solene came up behind her. She lifted Laney's hair into a twist atop her head. "Perhaps an updo. You can visit the resort's salon, or I can have hair, makeup and nail services sent to your villa."

"I'll wear my hair down, thank you."

"She doesn't wear makeup," Ian interjected, like this was a tedious conversation they'd had a hundred times.

Solene's eyes sprang wide. "Certainly, Mr. Luss. I was only concerned that Mrs. Luss might feel uncomfortable if she was underdressed in comparison to the other ladies who will be guests in the dining room tonight."

"Why don't we let my wife decide for herself? She isn't concerned with comparing herself to others." It wasn't a question. "Darling, would you like to change out of that dress for now? I'm sure Solene will have it sent to the villa."

Gussied up for dinner, Ian and Laney entered the resort's fine-dining restaurant. Located on the second story of one of the buildings, three of its walls were made of glass, so there was an unobstructed view of the waves under the setting sun.

Ian gestured to the bar, "Let's have a drink."

"Good evening. What can I get you?" The bartender welcomed them, wearing a white shirt with a colorful print bow tie.

"Shall we try something local?" Ian asked Laney.

She nodded.

The bartender said, "One of Bermuda's signature cocktails is the Rum Swizzle. May I prepare two of them for you?"

"Sounds yummy."

"Here at Pink Shores, we use two kinds of rum, light and dark, for the subtle difference in taste and depth." The bartender narrated as he made the drinks, beginning by adding ice to a stainless-steel mixing pitcher. "Orange juice and pineapple juice. Grenadine. A few dashes of bitters. You can imagine how the bitters will contrast the sweet juices and grenadine in a most refreshing way."

"I can't wait to try it," Laney said excitedly.

"The most important thing," the bartender said, "is the tradition of churning the drink. This makes it airy and frosty. We use a mixing spoon, but traditionally swizzles were used, which are thin stems from a tree grown in the Caribbean." He poured the drinks into tall glasses, garnishing each with a slice of pineapple, a slice of orange and a cherry.

"Ooh, it is frosty to the touch," Laney said as she took hers. After a small tasting sip, she smiled at the bartender. "This is delicious."

"I'm so glad you like it. I'd recommend having a seat." He pointed to groupings of tables that lined the front-facing glass wall. "We should have a beautiful sunset in about twenty minutes. Very romantic."

"Great," Ian said. "After all, that's what we're here for."

He put his arm around Laney's shoulder, as a beau might do, and in turn, she put hers around his waist. They were very easygoing by now. He moved, then she moved in response, just like dancing with a partner. He led her to a prime table with a 180-degree view of the water. He pulled out a chair for her and slid it closer to the table as she sat. So much like a dance that he didn't want the music to stop. He felt almost drunk before even taking a sip of his Rum Swizzle. Everything with Laney felt not only authentic but enthusiastic and alive and thrilling.

"This is truly paradise," Laney said as she took it all in.

Indeed.

She sipped her Rum Swizzle. "Where did you vacation as a child?"

"Oh, you know, rich people places. Summer on a yacht in the Greek islands, winter on the slopes of Aspen or the Alps. Made for great photos for the media."

"You didn't have a nice time?"

"It was fine. But I would sometimes look at other families who were being affectionate with each other and laughing all the time, sharing food from each other's forks in restaurants, and—I don't know, there's just a closeness between people that I've never felt."

Until her.

"You don't feel close to any of your family?"

"I love them dearly. I was closest to my

grandmother. But we're like a monarchy—formal. There weren't private moments that were just ours away from our image. No being curled around each other in front of the fireplace at Christmas, that sort of thing."

"That could be lonely."

Although no one in his family would have left a woman they'd impregnated to her own devices. "Were you happy as a child, Laney? It must have been difficult without a father."

"It was fine. I love my mom. That was what I knew. I didn't do well in school, although I think that was more the fault of the school than it was mine."

"What did your mother do for work?"

"She was a packer at a factory. It was hard on her back. Our world was small. That was why there was something for me about hanging out in cafés. They were places to stare into the middle distance. I would like sitting there imagining the lives of poets and astronauts and shipbuilders and grocery clerks, too. Thinking of the world as big."

They both reached for their drink at the same time, so Ian clinked her glass. Laney was endlessly interesting. He was used to the practicality of landowners and financiers in his orbit, not someone who talked of poets and daydreams.

Drink in one hand and fingers interlocking with the other, they looked out to one more of Bermuda's spectacular sunsets, just as the bartender had predicted it would be. The colors layered over the waves were truly awe-inspiring.

Finally, Ian said, "Too bad Melissa and Clayton missed out on this. It's a bang-up place for a honeymoon."

"Hey, we should call them, see how they're doing."

"Great idea."

Laney made a video call with her phone. Conveniently, both Melissa and Clayton were together. They were recuperating, and had managed to progress from their fare of plain toast and tea to applesauce and eggs. They'd decided not to come to Bermuda for the few days left on the trip, and would reschedule their honeymoon another time.

Laney tapped her phone, switching the camera lens to facing outward at the dazzling view. "Bermuda sure is nice!"

"Are you kidding me?" Melissa called out. "Showing me that is mean." But she giggled.

"We hate you," Clayton said, chiming in.

"Don't worry, it only looks like this when the sun goes down," Ian teased.

"In the morning," Laney added, "when the sun is coming up and the sky turns from a pale pink to white to the milkiest of blue, it's no big thing."

"You two are evil!" Clayton said.

"We have to go now. We're having dinner in the formal dining room where the walls are made of glass overlooking the ocean."

"Enjoy your applesauce," Laney said mischievously before ending the call.

"Your table is ready." The maître d' came to summon them as Laney was putting her phone in her purse.

"Ian Luss?" A booming voice from behind called his name.

"If you'll follow me." The maître d' gestured.

"Ian Luss!" The sound was so thunderous it echoed through the dining room. "What are you doing here?"

"Oh no," he whispered to Laney as he turned and recognized the barrel of a man as big as his voice, his jacket button straining to contain the whole of him. "Connery Whitaker."

"Who's that?" Laney hissed back as the

man approached with a snaky slip of a woman next to him.

"He's a fat-cat landowner from Maine," Ian said of the older man. "Luss Global has done business with him. A real blowhard."

"Ian Luss, Ian Luss." Connery stuck out his hand for a shake three feet ahead of reaching them. "Fancy meeting you here."

Ian met his hand with its corpulent pink fingers and accepted a comically robust handshake. "A surprise indeed."

"What are you doing at a couple's resort? I figured you for sewing wild oats in Beantown, taking all the hot young moneymakers in Boston for a ride."

He guided Laney closer to the conversation. "This is my...wife, Laney."

"Your wife, huh?" Connery regarded Laney with a leer from her cleavage to her toes. Then he spoke into Ian's ear but did a terrible job if he was intending for her not to hear. "You'll want to keep your options open with all the good-looking females at this resort. Nothing like a little honeymoon fling with another adventurous newlywed you get to say goodbye to afterward, if you know what I mean."

Ian mashed his lips, speechless.

Only then did Connery yank his companion into the fold. She was decades younger than him. Adorned with jewelry that looked like it could topple her over, she stuck out a hand as if for a shake and then decided not to bother and put her arm down.

"This is my new wife, Christie."

New wife? That sounded so off. Clearly the one that replaces the *old* wife. He wondered how many new models Connery had gone through.

"Nice to meet you." Ian forced a smile. He wasn't masking his discomfort with this chance encounter. He didn't need word getting back to the Boston finance community, or to anyone in his family, that he was spotted at a couples' resort in Bermuda.

Ian's eye caught the maître d', and he silently pleaded for help. Fortunately, he got the message. "Are you ready to be seated now, Mr. Luss?"

"Let's sit together," Connery announced rather than asked.

Ian whispered to the maître d', "Mr. Whitaker seems to be a bit tipsy."

"Understood, sir. Would you and Mrs. Luss like to follow me to your table? I'm sorry, Mr.

Whitaker, but we only have tables for two available tonight."

"It was nice to run into you, Connery," Ian said as he took Laney's hand and quickly pulled her away.

Connery husked to Ian again, not quietly enough to miss being heard. "Funny, Luss. I would have figured you for a beauty queen wife. Must be love?" He guffawed and shrugged his shoulders, which made the jacket button at his belly lift up as if it was ready to pop. "Ya just never know, huh?" His shrill laugh swirled in a circle.

Ian shut his eyes for a moment, as he knew how insulting and obnoxious that intrusion was.

They were seated at a window table near one of the modern chandeliers made of glass blown into the shape of a wave, which fit perfectly with the ocean-blue upholstery of the high-back dining chairs and island wood tables. He could tell Laney was still reeling from that awful Connery. The fun of teasing Melissa and Clayton over the phone seemed like it happened hours ago.

Nonetheless, Ian ordered a bottle of the best champagne, the sommelier poured a small taste for his approval, glasses were filled, and

Ian proposed a toast. "To the loveliest woman in the room." He tipped his glass toward her for a clink.

"As long as you don't care what work colleagues and personal shoppers think." She sniggered as she tapped her glass to his.

"I still say to the loveliest woman in the room."

She sighed at Ian's toast. "Can I order for us?"

"By all means. I eat everything under the sun."

"We'll start with the lobster and mango salad," Laney said when the waiter came. "Then we'll have the grilled wahoo. With that, we'll have jasmine rice and asparagus. And for dessert the Grand Mariner and dark chocolate soufflé."

"You don't fool around," Ian said.

She smiled.

As the first course of lobster was served, Ian asked, "At that café you're going to open, are you going to serve hearty food, or are you thinking of just the typical pastries and breakfast items?"

"I hope nothing I serve will be *typical*."

"Touché."

"I had the idea that I'd like to serve sand-

wiches and toasts with an international fla-
vor. Most cultures put something yummy on
top of bread. For example, an open-faced tar-
tine or a pressed sandwich with appetizing
grill marks on the bread. Yet uncomplicated.
I wouldn't have a restaurant kitchen."

"I was telling you about Café Emilia in
New York. They made clever use of their limited space by transforming an old wraparound
bar in the back of the room for their food stations. Same idea as what you're talking about,
just soups and pastries."

"I'll have to go see that someday."

"How about tonight?"

"What?"

"When we finish dinner. It will still be
early."

"It's in New York."

"It is." Ian pulled his phone out from his
pants pocket. After a few swipes and taps, he
announced, "A private plane will meet us in
an hour. We'll spend the night at the Hotel Le
Luxe. I booked a penthouse suite."

"Just like that?"

"Yes, just like that. Although perhaps we'll
cancel the soufflé and have dessert there."

CHAPTER NINE

"WELCOME TO NEW YORK," an attendant met Ian and Laney as they made their way down the boarding stairs after their small plane landed.

On cue, a limousine pulled right up on the tarmac, and a driver in a black suit and chauffeur's cap opened the passenger door for them to slide into the black butter-soft leather seat.

"I've taken the liberty of pouring some champagne," the driver said.

"Exactly where we left off in Bermuda." Ian noted that, per his instruction, the same champagne they were having with dinner was served to them in the limo.

"I still can't comprehend this," Laney said as she took the flute he offered. "The flight was like a blink, and now we're in New York. I didn't even change my clothes."

She was still in that attractive navy dress they'd bought earlier from the resort shop. Before they left for the flight, Ian suggested they quickly throw some things in a bag for the evening and morning, and then they'd take a flight to arrive back in Bermuda by lunch tomorrow. After all, they'd be eager to get back to their honeymoon.

He sensed Laney's breathlessness over the impromptu plans and was glad for it. Between that snooty saleswoman at the boutique and that awful Connery Whitaker they'd run into, he wanted her to have nothing but pleasure for the rest of the night. He really disliked that windbag, who was probably on his umpteenth wife and didn't have a clue how to treat a woman. That creature draped on his arm seemed uninterested in anything.

After just a bit of driving, Manhattan came into view, the glittering skyline with its skyscrapers and landmark buildings.

"The city never disappoints with its wow factor, does it?" said Ian.

"I've only ever approached it from a train, so I've never even seen it like this," said Laney.

When the driver parked in front of Café Emilia, he came around to open the door. "Here we are, sir."

"Just as I remembered it," Ian said and helped Laney out of the car.

She read the white cursive on the blue awning, "Café Emilia, Est. 1924." Then she looked up at the narrow red brick building, the second and third floors part of the café, window boxes displaying multicolored flowers.

"So here you are."

In between the two small outdoor patios was a heavy wood door, which he opened for Laney. They stepped inside.

She took a brisk inhale. "Smells so good. They roast their own coffee here."

"Freshly ground coffee, so aromatic."

The walls were covered with historic photographs in mismatched frames, the owner's family, celebrities and politicians, patrons over the years.

Laney moved toward some of the photos to get a better look. "I love it. Café life. Same as now." She swept her arm to gesture around at the room.

People sat on black metal parlor chairs around creaky wood tables, drinking, eating and talking. Larger groups sat on timeworn benches at long tables. The main room was huge and was divided into three seating sections.

"Between the din and the smell, it's like

stepping into history," said Laney. "What a scale this is on. So much management."

"I think later generations of the original family still run it."

"Let's see those." She moved toward a wood case that housed antique espresso machines and other equipment, some chrome and some bronze. "Look at the detailed metal work that went into making those urns. Some have the café's name on them."

"And this collection of coffee cups and saucers spanning the years."

"It's so loud and alive in here."

"How would you like to work in a place like this every day?"

"Nothing wrong with that! But I'd imagined my own place to be a wee bit smaller," she said jokingly.

"Here's what I wanted to show you." Ian cupped her elbow to lead her into the back of the crowded room.

A curved bar top, the counter made of marble with brass fittings on top of a solid wood foundation was probably where customers in the early days would be served a quick espresso.

"See how they use this as their sandwich bar," Ian said.

Laney pulled him backward so as not to be in the way of the staff, who were filling orders at breakneck speed.

"Yes, I see." She pointed to one area where a few cooks in chef's jackets were preparing deli sandwiches. "They have everything well laid out to make the assembly as efficient as possible."

"And over there."

"Old panini presses. Ooey gooey sandwiches with a nice crisp on the outside, lovely with a hot cup of coffee."

"And over there—" he pointed to another station with cooks hard at work "—they're making toast."

"It's all perfect." Along another area was a pastry case filled with selections. "This is great. I've always wanted to come here."

Laney smiled so genuinely it turned Ian's belly to mush. Elation sparkled over him like glitter. Making her happy was profoundly satisfying. Wasn't that what made life worth living? Creating and sharing joyous and meaningful moments, and recognizing them as such.

Ian wondered if his parents had those small flashes of light that added up to a profound contentment. If they did, it didn't show. He never saw enthusiasm or exuberance. Nothing unpleasant, either, only that the day-to-day was all they made room for. They didn't seem *un*happy. Perhaps they had everything they needed. They were able to play by the rules and live within the lines. Still, Ian couldn't help thinking that they only lived half-lives without knowing passionate love.

After Laney had her fill of looking around, he said, "Let's go upstairs."

He followed her as she climbed up the wrought iron spiral staircase.

"Oh, just as it looks in all of the photos I've seen!" she exclaimed when they reached the second floor. "Like someone's living room. Someone who collects old books, that is."

"Yes."

Wall-to-wall bookshelves held thousands of volumes. Dusty hardcovers and paperbacks with cracked spines. More books than the shelves could handle. They were crammed in vertically, horizontally and even diagonally as needed. Some of the shelves buckled from the weight. Stacks of more books with heavy glass slabs atop them created makeshift tables, surrounded by a hodgepodge of chairs and sofas, leather, wood, metal.

Most of the tables were filled with small

groupings of patrons involved in conversations as they bit into delectables from small plates and drank coffee. Cups with saucers and tiny espresso demitasse bore the current iteration of the café's name and logo, and tall glasses held milky recipes and frozen drinks.

"The vibe here is so excellent," Laney said, marveling. "Exactly how I thought it would be."

"Photos can only tell you so much. There's nothing quite like being here in person."

"I want to see the top floor."

Another go-round on the spiral staircase led them to a much smaller third-floor room furnished with larger tables and straight-backed chairs. This was the student haven.

In a sotto voice, she said, "I think customers respect that if you sit up here, it's meant as a quieter space."

"For people to read and write and study. It's lower key up here, but you can still hear all the city sounds coming in from the open windows."

"Well, we *are* in New York, after all."

Laney went to one of the open windows and peered down to the Greenwich Village streets. People of every kind bustled to and fro, young and old, local and tourist, student, career person, downtrodden, everyone.

"After this, can we go for a walk?" Laney asked.

"Your wish is my command." Ian Luss didn't generally talk like a lord from the Regency era. Laney had the oddest effect on him.

He was ready to break into a poem but managed to hold himself back. Crooning from the rowboat was enough. The point of this week was to get his longings out of his system. Instead, he was letting them *in*, and *out* was not going to happen without a fight. He'd better start now. He'd better start fighting right now...

He really was having that thought, to gain control and put the week in perspective, but once they stepped out of the café to the breezy, leafy evening, he kissed her. Another unscheduled kiss! That he promised both her and himself they weren't going to have more of. Yet he kissed her, a long passionate press that could not be misunderstood. And there was no denying that she kissed him back with equal zeal.

"Oh, no, again? We're supposed to stay away from each other." She giggled as she backed away from his mouth, making him lunge forward when she moved her head to the side to avoid the contact.

They both laughed.

"Walk, we were going to walk," Ian said.

They did, about twenty steps to a traffic intersection, where they had to wait for a green crossing light. And kiss. They had to kiss. As if it were the law.

"I have an idea," said Ian.

"What's that?" She slid her fingertips up and down along his arm, a sensation that was sent from heaven.

"I'll show you at the hotel." He tapped into his phone for the limo that came so quickly it was as if the driver was just around the corner.

They whirled uptown to reach the Hotel Le Luxe. With access activated from his phone, they rode a private elevator to the penthouse. The view from the suite of Central Park, its ground-level greenery and the tall buildings that bordered it was spectacular. The lavish layout, far more than they could utilize in one night, was furnished with fine black-and-white furniture, sage green accents and several fresh flower arrangements.

As soon as the door clicked shut, she toed off one shoe and then the other. Then she wrapped her arms around him and initiated another kiss, another five. She hushed into his ear, her mere tone making him twitch.

"What's your idea?"

"I was thinking," he answered in an otherworldly singsong, "and you don't have to agree. I was thinking that maybe the only hope for us is to take this honeymoon charade to its logical conclusion. We'll make love. Once and just once. That will put to rest the curiosity and temptation that we obviously feel. And then we'll have seen the fake honeymoon all the way through and be done with it. What do you think?"

It was as ludicrous as it sounded once he said it out loud.

But she slid her hands down to his waist and brought him closer to her. So close, in fact, that there was no space between them.

"Excellent idea."

What was Laney doing on the plushest mattress ever made in a penthouse suite at the Hotel Le Luxe in New York? She wasn't going to be able to reason out an answer to that. Because a gorgeous six-foot-plus Ian Luss, with lips that ought to be illegal, was laying on top of her, planting his mouth into the crook of her neck and making mental capabilities impossible.

"Ian," she managed to say.

"Yes?" His breath was hot against her skin.

"Don't stop doing what you're doing."

"I can't promise that."

"Why?"

"Because I might need to do this instead." He threaded his fingers into her hair and with his thumb lifted up her chin so that he could focus his slow kisses down the front of her throat, making her moan repeatedly.

"Ian," she cried, all but begging.

"I'm still here."

"It's that I don't want you to stop doing."

"This?" he teased with the tiniest bite at the base of her throat. And then he returned to the swerve of her neck, where his bite was bigger and more forceful. "Or that?"

"Yes."

"Yes, which?"

"Yes."

"Yes?"

"Yes."

And with that, he silenced the conversation, at least for the moment, by covering her lips with his, enveloping her with his arms and legs. His hands traveled from her face to her hips. Tugging up the skirt of the evening dress she still wore so that he could slide one hand between her bare legs, eliciting another desperate moan from somewhere far inside of her.

Meanwhile, her own hands wound around him on top of her to pull his shirt out from being tucked in his pants, needing similarly to feel his taut flesh in her palms.

"I think it's about time we get these clothes off. This is their second country in one day. They're tired."

He climbed off her, her whole being screaming at the loss, but knowing it was necessary. He unfastened the belt of her dress, satisfied to separate the two ends. Sliding his hands under her, he unzipped the back. From there, he was able to slip the dress over her shoulders and pull it down to reveal the silvery blue bra she'd worn underneath. Continuing his effort, he pulled the dress all the way down past the gray undies, along her legs and then off, tossing it to the bench beside the bed.

He cupped her breasts atop the smooth fabric covering them and deftly found the front clasp, which he was easily able to click open. He let out a gasp of pleasure that thrilled her to the bone as he held her bare breasts in his hands. He circled their contours, learning them, squeezing, buoying, pressing them together. He buried his face between them, tantalizing her with the slight scratch of stubble from his end-of-the-night facial hair. When his tongue flicked across one tight nipple, her head threw back on its own volition as current after current of yearning ran through her body.

"Oh," she piped, "I need to slow down."

"Of course."

"I want to savor every minute. Because we're only going to do this once."

"Yes. We want to get it right."

"Right," she repeated as she rolled on top of him, straddling his hips with one knee on either side of him and enjoying a slow unbuttoning of his shirt. Delighting in palming a few more inches of his solid chest with each button's release. Reveling in his arousal between her legs. She finally glided the shirt off him.

His hands went to her shoulders, and he flipped them so that he was on top of her again, where she was grateful that more of their naked flesh touched each other than before. Back to that path he was forging down the column of her throat, and this time going farther, between her breasts, down her rib-cage to the elastic band of her undies. Where he stopped to deliver a million and a half tiny kisses, making her desperate for his mouth to go farther, to know more. At long last his tongue slid under the fabric, where he kissed across one hipbone and then to the other, intoxicating her with his patterns, sending her into an elated state she'd never been in before.

Just when she thought she couldn't stay still a moment longer, he bit into the gray silk of the underwear and used his teeth to drag them off her. With her sex uncovered for him to see, he used both of his hands to part her legs and then began another of his trails of kisses up the inside of one leg to her very center. Using the tip of his tongue to coax her open, she relaxed her legs and welcomed his attention. He made her bloom, opening and welcoming him more with his slow circles up one side and down the other. He varied the pressure of his tongue from barely making contact to long deliberate licks, occasionally rearing his head back to monitor the pleasure on her face as her eyelashes fluttered.

Her core clenched, contracting and releasing, contracting and releasing as his able tongue measured her responses. When the squeezing became more frequent, he slowed down, helping her prolong the inevitable. Finally, she couldn't hold on and went over the edge, free-falling as her body trembled and quaked while he kept his tongue in her. Then he held her and patiently waited until she stilled.

When she did, her hands appreciatively slid down his sides and then inward to the fly of his pants, where she quivered at the hardness inside. She unhooked the tab, released the zipper and, a bit to one side and then the other, inched them off him, along with the boxer briefs he wore underneath. His hips thrust forward, begging her hands to explore, and they eagerly obliged. His sex throbbed, and she knew the next thing she needed was to have him inside of her. He leaned away long enough to grab a condom from his bag, and she watched as he fit it onto himself.

He crawled back on top of her. His mouth took hers greedily. "I have to have you."

"Be inside me," she said, concurring.

She'd been through so much with him already. The kinship they'd developed. The open conversation, the confiding in each other, the frankness about their lives and their positions and their goals. This was the obvious next step, to learn each other this way, to know each other from the inside. She wanted this, too. Once.

Years from now, tonight would remain one of the defining moments of her life. This gorgeous, brilliant, distinguished man had shared this interlude with her, the week in Bermuda, the pretend honeymoon, this spontaneous overnight to New York, and now this carnal joining. He wasn't Ian Luss of Luss Global Holdings and the constrictions that implied. And she wasn't Lumpy Laney from Dorchester. They were something much higher, much more elemental. They were man and woman. Light and dark. Hot and cold. Heart and soul. Sun and moon. Husband and wife.

It wasn't her fate to have him forevermore even if she was able to. He was only a moment in space and time that she hadn't known she needed. To make her feel hungered for, to put distance between her and the past. Most unexpectedly, they were thrown together to help each other get to where they were going next. Sent from providence for that purpose alone. And that was okay.

He needed to process his genuine torment about romantic love that he wasn't going to carry with him into his family-approved future. For her, he was a gift from the heavens, the recharge that came in a surprise package and would only stay a short while. Although a hunch within her knew it wasn't going to be so easy to say goodbye.

With an even greater level of need, he positioned his body on top of her. In one thrust he entered her sex, which was wet and waiting for him. It didn't surprise her body that he was a perfect fit, shifting into place, to where he belonged.

They rocked together as one being, coming almost apart but then pushing back together, as if their bodies couldn't withstand a full separation. With hips swirling and undulating, they danced a waltz they needed no lesson for, as their bodies somehow knew it already. The music their ears heard intuited how to dance toward the crescendo, the full articulation, the culmination, as the cymbals crashed together into ecstasy.

It was still the deepest black of the New York sky that reflected from the tall buildings when Ian looked out the windows. He'd already sat up, swiped open his phone and was putting the plan he'd devised during the night into play. Once done, he studied Laney beside him on the bed, asleep, resting her head on the palatial hotel pillows. A tug pulled at him from the sight of her like that, almost childlike in her peace, each breath filling her with slumber. She was almost too captivating to wake up. However, he had somewhere to take her.

Leaning over, his fingers couldn't resist threading through her hair and smoothing back the strands that had fallen forward. Her eyelashes flickered a bit. The back of his hand caressed her cheek until she woke enough to smile in acknowledgement of his contact.

"Why are you awake?" she cooed.

"We're going out."

"Wonderful idea. In a couple of hours."

She started to roll as if she were going to turn her back to him. Kisses to the top of her shoulder stopped her.

"No. Now."

"No." She laughed. "Later."

"It's urgent."

"Nothing could be that urgent."

"Okay." He buried his face into her hair and could see her point in refusing to leave the comfort of the bed. "You're going to miss the big surprise."

"Surprises are appreciated during daylight,

too." He began administering little suction kisses up and down her neck that he knew would be annoying. He was successful.

She giggled and said, "Stop that!"

"Only if you get up." He pushed the blankets to the side, revealing her glorious nudity.

"Grar!" She made a funny grunt that sounded like it was coming from an old man, but she did get out of bed. "How am I supposed to dress for this surprise?"

"What you're wearing is fine."

All she had on was a little bit of perfume lingering from the night before. Which she didn't even need, because he adored the fragrance of her skin. Of her hair. The taste of her mouth. And of every part of her. Which he'd explored thoroughly and could have been ready to start again from the top and work his way down.

"Very funny."

"We brought jeans and jackets. It might be cold out right now."

"Where are we going before dawn, anyway?"

"You'll find out soon enough."

They rode the private elevator down to the hotel lobby, which was almost empty except for a couple of groups with luggage beside them, perhaps leaving for an early flight. The driver he'd booked was waiting outside as arranged, and Ian and Laney got into the back seat of the town car.

After a quick ride to the border of Central Park, the driver pulled over, and they exited.

"We're going to the park?"

"In a way." He held out the crook of his arm for her to take as he walked her away from the sidewalk and into the grassy dampness.

"What's happening?"

"Over there."

Illuminated by the milky glow of an old-fashioned lantern as morning mist began to lighten the sky, a man dressed in a top hat, black tailcoat and a plaid scarf sat in an open-air carriage led by a white horse. Ian couldn't manage any internal cool at all as they approached. A horse-drawn carriage at dawn was such a silly and cliché symbolism of romance. He was already loving every damn minute and was so glad he'd thought of it.

"What is this?" Laney tilted her head quizzically as he led her toward the carriage, the horse in its magnificence draped with a red satin cloth.

"Milady." The driver hopped down from his seat, crossed his hand around his midsection to bow forward at the waist, extending one foot into a pointed toe that would have been at home on a Broadway stage. "I am Farrell, and my horse's name is Sonny. We are at your service."

"We're going on a carriage ride?" Laney was flabbergasted, which brought a satisfied smile to Ian's lips. He wanted to dazzle her, and he seemed to have succeeded.

"Milady, would you like to get to know Sonny? Perhaps give him a snack?" Farrell pulled a carrot out of a sack and handed it to her.

She didn't hesitate and went right to the horse, with his pristine white coat, and fed him the carrot. Giving a gentle pet down the length of his face, she said, "Hello, Sonny. It's nice to meet you."

After a few minutes with him, Farrell suggested they get going. He brought Laney to the side of the carriage and saw to it that she hoisted herself safely up the step and into the carriage seat. Then Ian joined her. He made a fuss of unfolding a plaid flannel blanket over their laps. Farrell pointed to a picnic hamper on the floor beneath them. "Everything you ordered, sir."

Then they were on their way, *clippetty-*

clopping into the almost-silence of the park. Ian opened the hamper to find a large thermos, which he opened. He poured steaming liquid into the two heavy black ceramic mugs, which bore drawings of the carriage on them.

"Hot chocolate." He handed her one.

Off they went through the paths between trees, the sky opening more with every trot the horse took. Daylight was starting to grace the sky with a pale blue glow. The air smelled fresh and woodsy.

"Ian, I can't believe you thought of doing this."

"Honestly, I can't, either."

He reached into the hamper to pull out a crystal bowl filled with bright red strawberries. He wasted no time in feeding her a berry, enjoying in great detail her comely lips opening to accommodate the fruit.

"My turn," she teased and dipped her finger into the bowl to take one.

As she brought it to his lips, the veins in his body coursed with awareness. She put him through an exquisite pace by running the end of the strawberry slowly across his top lip and then around to his lower, making a full circle before feeding it to him. He bit in. It was as sweet and juicy as he knew it would be.

"This is fun."

"I'm glad you think so."

As the carriage passed the park's carousel, wordless without children in the sunlight of day, he dug into the hamper again to pull out a box of the tiny cupcakes he'd ordered. He chose a lemon one and brought it to her mouth, letting her think he was going to feed her the bite-size confection. But instead, he swiped his finger to get the frosting, which he painted across her lips, just as she'd done with the strawberry. Only he took it further and licked the sugary cream straight from her, thinking that was possibly the most delicious thing he had ever tasted. A little sigh of approval escaped her lips. He could imagine listening to both her laughter and her sounds of pleasure for the rest of his life.

Which brought up an interesting point, he thought to himself. The more he lived out these acts of romance, the more he wanted them. Her. It wasn't simply the idea of romance he was enchanted with. It was Laney. He didn't know why or how, but he knew he wanted her beside him and to be beside her. He didn't know how he was going to keep to their nonsensical pact to make love only once to rid themselves of the curiosity and then be done with it. This whole getaway had been so magical, so divine, he knew something absolute had happened. That he wanted to be only with her and for the rest of his life. It wasn't going to be merely hard to part when the honeymoon was over. It was going to be next to impossible, like having to leave his soul behind.

While his arm wrapped around Laney's shoulder, Farrell guided the carriage toward the Sheep Meadow section of the park, so named because actual sheep roamed the vast lawn a century ago. Sonny trotted through the paths that were populated only by a few early morning joggers. Ian felt as if they were galloping away from something and toward something new. As Sonny brought them closer to the Bethesda Terrace and Fountain, Ian heard the sound he was expecting as it seeped through the thick of the sunrise.

Laney turned her head for her ears to chase the sound she couldn't exactly make out. She asked, "What am I hearing?" When they got a little closer the sound came into focus. "Is that a violin?"

"Can you make out the song?"

She sang out the notes as she put it together. "What I want is right there. We were meant as a pair. Oh, it's 'Meant as a Pair.' From the wedding. And you sang it on the rowboat. How can that be?"

When they got to the terrace, she could see that a violinist stood in the shadows of dawn wearing a coat and tie, coaxing the melody from his strings.

"How could he be playing that song?"

"You mean *our* song?" He sang, "I would walk without fear. Every moment we share."

"Did you arrange this?"

"Of course."

"Oh, Ian." She brought her hand over her mouth. Tears welled in her eyes.

Farrell slowed the carriage to a stop.

Ian hopped out and then helped Laney down. He brought her closer to the music, each note resonant, almost weeping from the lone instrument. Then he placed his arm around her waist and began to lead them in a dance.

The violinist played on, accompanied by the morning hush.

"We know how to do this now," he murmured into her ear. "All of it."

Indeed they did, had learned how each other's bodies moved and reacted. In the penthouse bed as well as now. Inside the intimacy of the moment. In New York at dawn. They danced. Just them.

"Ian, for an anti-romantic, you sure know how to woo a girl."

CHAPTER TEN

"THAT WAS THE most incredible experience of
my life." Laney gushed from her plane seat.
She was holding the bouquet of purple asters
that the carriage driver Farrell presented to
her when the ride was over. That, of course,
Ian had arranged.

He pointed out the window as the plane as-
cended into the skies. "The Empire State Building."

She watched until the landmark building
was obscured from view by the clouds. Ian
squeezed her hand in a gesture she could only
interpret as togetherness.

"Really, Ian, I want to acknowledge everything you did to make this overnight to New
York so special. It's the nicest thing anyone
has ever done for me."

A wide smile cracked across his mouth.
His grin, coupled with the sparkle in his eyes,
made her gulp.

"I'm glad you enjoyed it so much. It was fun for me, too. Really. Really fun."

Although, plane rides and horse-drawn carriages and throwing money on wild things wasn't going to solve his real problem, which was how he was going to live day after day, year after year, without being true to himself. To who he was.

"You know, I think you're going to have to work a little romance into that *strictly business* marriage you keep talking about. It's in your makeup, you can't deny it."

His eyes shot to the middle distance, a bit of a sad pallor taking over his face.

She hated that she'd broken his smile. "I'm sorry, did I say the wrong thing?"

"No, no, it's fine," he said distractedly. "I'm just glad we have a couple of days more in Bermuda before the week is out."

"Yeah." Laney chewed her lip.

The mood in the private plane's small cabin had turned melancholy. Could he have been thinking what she was? That maybe making love was a mistake. Making heart-pounding, all-encompassing, heavenly love put them in jeopardy. Because in Bermuda at the resort, they were pretending to be a couple. Alone at the pond, they'd had no such obligation. Or in New York at the café. Or at the penthouse. Where they were merely Laney and Ian. They didn't have to convince anyone they were together. There was no reason what happened had to happen. Except that it had.

"What would you like to do when we get back to the island?"

She could tell he was making small talk. That was fine. She'd welcome getting out of her own head, worrying about what she was going to miss that wasn't real in the first place.

"Maybe not on a rowboat, but being in the water as much as possible. I'm not in the water much in Boston. Are you?"

"Not in town. But my family meets out at the vineyard fairly often. We have a compound there." A compound at Martha's Vineyard. Of course, the Luss family has a *compound*.

She could only imagine, an enormous piece of property with both developed and undeveloped portions. A mansion with a swimming pool and tennis courts, maybe a private beach or dock. Outbuildings, guest houses and dedicated entertaining spaces, a band shell, gardens, animals.

Soon, he'd be returning to a life she could hardly conceive of. She wouldn't see him again unless they were invited to something by Melissa and Clayton. There was nothing between them except this week of fantasy and pretending. And not pretending.

What lay ahead for her when the week was over was quite something else. She had to get a job as soon as possible and find an apartment she could afford so that she didn't overstay her welcome at Shanice's. She had to build up again. That was okay. Her mission was clear. Once she found a job, starting as a barista or in lower management, she'd begin jockeying for a higher position. Maybe a night job, too, so she could start saving money for the big dream of ownership. On her own. As it should be. None of that was the problem.

She looked over to the problem. The cut of his jaw was tight, maybe even forced. His upright body was filled with tension. All muscle strength and posture. Fighting to not be the Ian who danced with her at sun up while the violinist played their song. *Their* song.

She choked back tears. Because in the time they'd shared together so far this week, there had been many shards of sunshine when he'd let her see not Ian Luss the billionaire who would find that serviceable marriage. No, in the wisps between dusk and twilight, between sips of morning coffee, between rowboats and

New York and dancing foibles, he'd let her see who he really was. And she'd done the same. And now that she had, it wasn't something she ever wanted to stop doing.

This one man had the power to dissolve all the hurt she thought she'd carry with her for the rest of her life. Even if he could, would she let him? Would she take the chance? It was never to be, so the questions didn't need answering.

With seemingly nothing to provoke it, they exchanged a heartfelt smile as Hamilton came into view, neither saying any of what was going through their minds. Because, in a way, there was nothing to say. They both knew the laws. And to stop breaking them. Better that they just kept smiling and creating memories to hold on to. Why not continue to enjoy the grand masquerade when they got back to the resort? They held hands as the plane touched ground. She could do this.

The Bermuda day was glorious with sultry breezes. As soon as they got to the villa, they put on swimsuits and ran down those stairs that led straight into the water.

"I've got you," Ian growled as he grabbed her once they reached the bottom.

Picking her up, he flung her around until

she could straddle his back and wrap her arms around his neck and her legs across his waist, piggyback style. He carried her farther into the water until he could swing her back again, this time cradling her in his arms. She sighed up at him as he held her, the sun behind his handsome face while he gazed down on her.

As long as she didn't let those thoughts of permanence blur the beautiful picture she was staring up at, of him looking down at her in warmth and approval and joy, there was no problem. She was just going to enjoy these last couple of days in paradise with him and then get on with her life. No problem. None at all.

"Good evening, Mr. and Mrs. Luss." Concierge Adalson waved to them as he passed by on a golf cart. "You're leaving us tomorrow?"

"Sadly, we are." Ian nodded.

"I hope you had a wonderful honeymoon."

"We did." Laney's voice was a little wobbly, but the concierge wouldn't have caught it.

They strolled the palm path near their villa, breathing in the early evening cool, admiring a flower here and there. It was their last night in Bermuda.

A housekeeper they'd seen a few times

called out as she wheeled her cart, "Is there anything special I can leave in your villa for your final night with us?"

"We're fine, thank you," Laney answered.

Fittingly, they also saw the older couple they'd first seen on the plane from Boston. The two putted golf balls on a small green, and both waved as the Lusses went by.

Yes, they had become quite comfortable at Pink Shores. They were friendly and polite and were clearly in love. The staff had done everything they could to make sure their honeymoon was memorable and pitch perfect. Ian was certainly going to miss being here when they went home to Boston tomorrow.

He put his arm around his bride's shoulder, and she followed suit by wrapping her arm around his waist, motions they both performed automatically now. She wore a long and loose floral print dress that they'd picked up at one of the resort shops, her hair wild and free, her skin clean. Ian had on a simple blue T-shirt and jeans. His brain and central nervous system were still swooning from the encounter in the water a couple of hours ago, although showering and dressing for the evening helped him balance out. He was planning to appreciate every minute of their last evening together.

Besides, what had happened on the steps leading from the villa to the water didn't mean anything. When they'd first arrived almost a week ago, a wicked fantasy had overtaken him of laying Laney down on the bottom of the staircase and making love to her in a way that half of their bodies were submerged in water and half above it. With the private beach, the greenery and tall hedges giving them complete privacy, it was practically possible.

But at the beginning of the trip, he never could have imagined that they would have joined their bodies in rapture and rhapsody the way they had in New York. They'd agreed not to do it again, that it was an extra complication that they didn't need as the week came to an end. The resolve lasted for a couple of days and nights despite all the time spent romping in the water.

Then, earlier today, before he'd made a conscious decision to fulfill that specific fantasy, he was doing it, lifting her up again in his arms and laying her down at the bottom of the stairs, making short work of removing the black triangles of fabric covering the few inches of her body.

Hovering over her, he kissed every inch he could get his hands and mouth on before sliding into her and wrapping her legs around him. The cool waves that reached the stairs lapped over them, crashing gently onto their legs and across his back. Soon, they found the ocean's rhythm and joined it, moving along with the ebb and flow of each wave. He thrust into her as the sea crashed atop them and then he retreated, back arched, as the water receded. They repeated with the tide about a hundred times, because it felt that glorious. His lovely Laney, the Bermuda waters, all under the setting sun. For the last time.

The bartender put two cocktail napkins printed with the resort's logo in front of them as they entered the outdoor cocktail lounge. "What can I get you?"

"The other day we tasted the Rum Swizzle, the bartender mentioned another cocktail famous in Bermuda."

"Yes, the Dark 'n' Stormy."

"Two of those, please."

"Coming right up. This drink mixes ginger beer with dark rum. We pour it over ice and garnish with a slice of lime."

"It sounds wonderful," Laney said, approving.

"Ian Luss, we meet again." Connery charged

toward them, the rail-thin Christie in tow. Oddly, a photographer trailed behind, a gangly young man with three cameras around his neck.

"Connery." Ian saluted with two fingers to his forehead, then pivoted back to the bar, hoping the bothersome man would go away.

No such luck in getting rid of him, of course. "I'm having some honeymoon shots done and figured it'd be cute to pose with a couple of the local cocktails. Bartender, fix us up something with lots of straws and umbrellas."

The bartender nodded and tried to conceal the speck of annoyance that washed over his face.

Ian had no choice but to rotate toward Connery again. "Nice idea." Maybe if he just responded to questions with short answers and didn't attempt to get a conversation going, Connery would move on.

The bartender presented the two drinks to Connery.

He grabbed them without any acknowledgment and handed one to his bride with such haste that a bit of it spilled over onto the ground, which he took no notice of. "Ian, let's get a couple of shots of the four of us."

"Oh, no, thanks, Connery. We're commemorating in our own way."

Ian didn't like Connery in general. In the few dealings he had with him, Ian found him too aggressive and unwilling to compromise. But what he really hadn't liked was when they'd run into each other a few days ago, he'd made some comment about assuming Ian would marry a *beauty queen type*. It was a slight at Laney that was in bad taste. Who would make a negative comment about a man's wife? On his honeymoon, no less!

What constituted a beauty queen wife, anyway? Purely beauty. And how was beauty defined, how was it not subjective? It was truly in the eyes of the beholder. From his view, Laney was absolutely lovely in her naturalness. Not to mention, it was her inner beauty that attracted him to her. It was a revolting thought that Laney's ex thought she should go under a surgeon's knife to add a *lilt* to her nose, to change an act of Mother Nature, who never made mistakes.

The way the sunshine reflected in Laney's eyes. Was there a measurement for that? And her kisses that took him to a jubilation he never wanted to return from. Did that have a numeric value? Not to mention the utter splendor of making love with her, feeling himself inside of her unimaginable lushness. Would that win a contest? To him, she was both a *beauty* and a *queen*.

In any case, Connery was so tactless that Ian couldn't wait to get away from him.

"Come on, Ian, what's the harm? Take a couple of shots with us," Connery insisted. He didn't wait for an answer as he grabbed Laney by the arm and asked, "What was your name again?"

"Laney." She forced a smile.

Ian was one move away from physically separating him from her. Meanwhile, Connery used his other arm to yank his wife over, which left Ian no choice but to join the foursome for the photo. He'd take a quick snap and then be done with it. At Connery's lead, they all held up their drinks and smiled.

"To happy marriages. Of course, mine is my third, but maybe three's a charm." He guffawed with a belly laugh. He turned to Laney and asked, "What was your name again?"

"We did it," Ian said as he held Laney's naked body against his own. "Our week as Mr. and Mrs. Luss comes to an end."

"In our marital bed." She laughed lightly

against his chest. "I think we were quite convincing."

"Think of where we started."

"With the pillow fortress between us. Followed by you on the sofa."

"I was gentleman enough to not tell you how uncomfortable that was."

As Ian's fingertips traced Laney's breasts, she hoped he wouldn't stop the motion anytime soon. It was like he was painting her with the pads of his fingers, and she wanted to be covered by his color.

"Did the separation work for you?" Laney asked.

"No. I was thinking about what you were, or weren't, wearing," he said.

"Nothing."

"That's what I was afraid of."

"Yay for us, though."

"Yes, we were able to get to this," he said. "We explored what we wanted to together, and now we can part without wondering what might have been."

"And I would have, you know." She splayed her hand on his sturdy chest, letting the muscles underneath his skin imprint into her hand, solidifying another memory.

"I would have, too."

"Now we know."

"We took our masquerade to its ultimate conclusion."

"I came to relax and pull myself together after the fire and the creep."

"Did you?"

"I feel rejuvenated."

"Mission accomplished, then."

"And you? Are you ready to go find that proper wife?" Even though she was trying to be casual and cavalier, it hurt Laney to even say those words out loud. Because, in her heart—and she believed in his, too—the right partner for him had already been found.

He said only, "Now we'll part ways and get on with our lives."

"Exactly."

"Although, I bet we'll see each other again."

"Of course. Through Melissa and Clayton," Laney said.

"We'll be friendly at holiday parties," said Ian.

"Give each other a polite kiss on the cheek."

"After all, we were best man and maid of honor. That always makes a special bond."

"Everyone will laugh about the bride and groom and the bad oysters that launched the Great Bermuda Charade," said Laney.

"Maybe Melissa and Clayton will ask us to be godparents to their children someday."

"It could happen."

"But this will never happen again," Ian said.

"Neither of us would want it to," said Laney.

"It doesn't fit with our schemes."

"We knew that from the start."

"We are pointed in different directions," said Ian.

"Couldn't be more different."

"Couldn't."

And with that, Ian rolled on top of her, his magnificent weight bearing onto her, enclosing her. Sparking her yet again, *yet again*, with want.

Her arms circled his neck, hands feeling for his upper back, bringing him in closer to her, never close enough, sealing them together making sure they became one. Until…

"No more," she blurted suddenly.

He immediately moved off, not making her struggle.

"I can't do it anymore. I can't pretend this week didn't mean anything," said Laney.

His Adam's apple bounced as he resigned his back against the pillows beside her. "It meant everything."

"You've given me back the possibility of

love. You've given me myself. You…" She couldn't say what came next. That part would have to stay in Pretend Land, a place that could never be.

They both knew that. Because he'd done more than just show her that love would be worth fighting for. Something that she'd wanted and had recently convinced herself she wouldn't have.

She still wouldn't. Because the lucky woman who would get to spend her lifetime with him would never get to see what Laney had this week. He was determined that no one would see what he was capable of.

"This week will be inside of me for the rest of my life," Ian said.

She blew out her cheeks and then let out a slow exhale. "So where does this leave us?"

"Nowhere." His answer felt like a blow.

The rowboat on the pond and the carriage ride in New York. Scenes from movies or his imagination come to life. Bursting from the black-and-white screen in his mind into the here and now. Will that be how he'll remember her, as an actress in the play he wrote? Making her wonder if he'd really been with *her* this week, or would any willing woman have been able to assume the role? That was an unbearable possibility.

Instead, she'd remember the special rapport they had with each other. How precious he made her feel.

She'd mentally thank him every day of her life for helping her choose the right path out of the crossroads she found herself in. She could have fallen into a pit, let events of the past trap her and hold her down. He gave her the confidence and the hope to pull herself back up. She'd make him proud, tell him of her gratitude every morning when she woke up and every night when she went to bed. She suspected he wouldn't be far from her thoughts anyway.

Yet his march toward the future was clear. It couldn't include her. He'd remain loyal to his family and she respected him for it. It made him the noble and trustworthy man he was. Even if he was her destiny, she was not his. What a cruel twist of fate that was.

Still, she wouldn't have traded this week for anything in the world. Because she'd always have it. It would affect everything she did, said, thought and felt until her dying day.

CHAPTER ELEVEN

MULTIPLE SPARKS OF emotion were fighting each other for Ian's attention after the plane's wheels lifted up to fly him and Laney off Bermuda and back to Boston. The obvious one was that he didn't want to leave that pink sand and the sunrises and sunsets that touched him with their magnificent display of colors. Another was that he'd grown quite used to spending almost every moment with Laney, who stared absently out the window while holding the cup of coffee she'd been handed but had yet to bring to her lips.

They'd supposedly said all that needed saying to each other. That in an uncomplicated world, they might try to be together. She might be able to trust again. Ian might fulfill his heart's desire to truly be in love with someone and to display it in every way possible. Not just with anyone. With her. Those were all *mights*. That was talk; it wasn't what was going to be. Instead, they agreed to part smiling and cherish this unforgettable interlude forever.

Except that Ian wanted to toss all of that *should do* crap and smash it against a wall until it shattered into a thousand pieces!

And once the pilot made the plane's Wi-Fi available, things got infinitely worse. Numbly scrolling through a Boston news site, his thumbs froze when he saw the photo. He and Laney and Connery Whitaker and his wife Christie. From when they ran into each other last night and that buffoon Connery insisted they take a jolly photo together. He told Ian he was documenting their trip. In fact, he made a production of ordering tropical drinks and posing with them. A click-through button on the screen said Read More.

"Laney." Ian summoned her attention, as they might as well bite the bullet together. He hit the button. "Look at this."

"What is it?" She put her cup down on the tray and leaned in to him so they could both see the phone at the same time.

"Is Ian Luss, one of the city's most eligible bachelors, off the market?" he read aloud.

"Ick."

He continued: "It seems it won't be a daughter of society that will join the Luss empire. Apparently, Ian's independent woman eschews high heels in favor of wearing an apron and pulling espresso. Records identify her as last co-owning a small café in the Berkshires. Laney Sullivan isn't a name known in the upper circles, which has left readers dumbfounded as to how this seemingly odd couple got together."

"Oh my gosh."

"That's infuriating." Ian put his hand over his chest as his rib cage collapsed. "It's sick that people want to read trash like that."

He wanted to scream. Because gossip about him wasn't embarrassing enough. No, they had to drag Laney into it. With all she'd been through and that idiot Enrique making her feel less than. This perpetuated that exact same message. Who was worthy enough to marry. Who was acceptable to love. As if that was for someone else to decide. One of Boston's most eligible bachelors. Nauseating.

"Do you think…" Laney's spoke slowly because she was in shock, too "…Connery sent the photos to the site himself?"

"I wouldn't put it past him."

"It could have been some other onlooker who recognized you."

"Spilled milk at this point."

"I suppose."

The flight attendant returned, rightly oblivious to the shake-up he and Laney were reckoning with. She laid down a tray that had several compartments, all filled with snacks for the short flight. The dried fruits had a glisten, the nuts looked nicely roasted and seasoned, the grapes big and juicy.

Ian had no interest in eating. Laney looked the tray over with ambivalence as well. They sat in silence until it became unbearable.

"I'm so sorry, Laney. I failed to protect you."

"Was that your job?"

"It might have been."

Yes, he wanted to shield her from harm, both physically and emotionally. He wanted her surrounded only by people who supported her, who saw how smart and decent she was. How true to herself. He could still kick himself remembering when he'd suggested she might want to fix her hair at the wedding after it had gotten mussed. Not that she wouldn't have wanted to look her best, but why would anyone want to change someone as glorious as her? Her honesty shone in her face. He loved everything about her.

Wait...loved? Was this what being in love really felt like? Pain and agony? He didn't know exactly how love informed the carrier. Was it the buzz he felt when he was near her? Or was it the burning, distracting longing when he wasn't? Was it the overwhelming impulse to defend her against any foe, including his family's and society's expectations? Was it in looking forward to the next day, sharing an adventure and discoveries made together?

Poets and painters had their ways of interpreting romantic love, of declaring it. Ian didn't know how to label it. Because all he'd ever known was that he was supposed to avoid it. Had it defied him, found him in the crowd anyway? Had it crept into the cracks of the cement wall holding him back?

He wasn't sure whether to lament or rejoice.

A limo met Laney and Ian at the airport in Boston. They slid into the back seat, the usual champagne and chocolates at the ready. She thought *the usual* because, remarkably, that's what the week had brought. Every single luxury imaginable at the resort, a private plane, the finest everything. She didn't know whether she could ever get used to so much opulence. At the moment, it didn't really matter. The driver was speeding them toward goodbye, and that would be that.

She kept her eyes looking out the window because she was at the point where being with Ian was stinging like a wound. They'd already expressed they wished that things could be different, that they could continue to explore the compatibility and bliss they felt toward each other. They couldn't. Period. She would be grateful to Ian for the rest of her life for showing her that a good man wasn't like Enrique. A good man wanted the best for his woman, accepted and nurtured her, didn't try to bring her down to inflate his own ego.

"I can't apologize enough for that ridiculous Connery and those photos and captions."

"Yeah." She pulled out her phone to torment herself with them again.

Just look at your face! she wanted to scream at Ian. He was so alive in those photos, with the most genuine grin as he held an arm around her. They were the perfect newlyweds, giddy in each other's company, the promise of a lifetime together in their eyes.

In a second photo, Ian looked at her with such awe, like she was the most heaven-sent thing he'd ever laid eyes upon. Didn't he see it, too, that by letting her go he was giving up on the very essence of who he was? How could duty make up for that? What his family was asking of him was too extreme, too unjust.

As requested, the driver brought her to Shanice's apartment building with the overflowing trash cans in front and the graffiti on the building next door. Three young men walking down the street stopped to gawk, as a limo was rarely seen in these parts.

"This is where you're staying?" Ian had obviously never lived in a neighborhood like this.

"I grew up a couple of blocks from here. This is me."

The driver pulled over to the curb and retrieved her luggage. It wasn't much, the small bag that she'd taken straight from the wedding onto the plane to Bermuda and the second containing what she'd acquired during the trip. The bathing suits. The navy evening dress. The heartbreak.

"Can I carry these up for you?" Ian pointed to them.

"No, I'm fine. It's only three flights of

stairs." Her eyes pooled, and she battled not to let any drops out.

"I'm so sorry about…everything."

"Not your fault." Again, she wanted to yell at him, wanted to shake his shoulders. He was completely missing the point. She didn't care about the photos and being described with unflattering words by his colleague and the press. The way Ian made her feel was far more important than what some gossip website thought. He'd shown her that it was worth it to trust. That not only could she open her heart again, that she wanted to. She said softly, "I'll see you around sometime."

Even though she said she didn't need help, he swooped up the bags and headed toward the five-step stoop that led to the front door of the building.

Laney followed and used her key to open the door.

He elbowed it wide. "Sure you don't want me to come up?"

"No. I'll be fine." She took the bags from him.

"Laney, it was a time…" He couldn't finish.

"Yeah." She cracked a wry half smile. "It was a time."

She headed up the stairs and didn't hear

the front door click shut until she got to the third floor.

As soon as she let herself in, she rushed to the window to see him climb into the limo's back seat.

Come back! Follow your heart! Choose me! she pleaded, although she didn't really. She only silently mouthed the words.

Watching the limo drive away, she finally let the tears that had been waiting spill down her cheeks. She was hurt and she was furious. That he couldn't do it. He couldn't choose her. He couldn't choose love.

She spent the next week traipsing all over Boston. Streets she'd known her whole life looked unfamiliar now. Dismal. Lonely.

She walked in Boston Common, the oldest park in America, and thought about the garden groves of the Pink Shores Resort with Ian. She ambled through the Freedom Trail, the path tourists always visited with its sights that tell the history of the United States. The harbor where Americans dumped hundreds of chests of tea into the water as a political protest.

She strolled on the Charles River Esplanade, thinking of when she and Ian fell into that pond and kissed for the first time. One day, she lingered in front of the Fletcher Club, where Melissa and Clayton's wedding took place, looking up to the windows as if there were something to see.

She spoke to Melissa on the phone and tried not to be too obvious in her probing to learn if she or Clayton had heard from Ian. Neither had.

Fortunately, after only a week, she was able to find a job as an assistant manager at a café a few blocks away from Shanice's apartment. It was a funky independent like she preferred, not part of a big chain that had a uniform way of doing everything. It was owned by a nice family.

Because she wasn't going to be making enough money to get a place of her own, Shanice agreed to let her share the rent for a couple of months. They reconfigured the living room with a standing divider so that Laney had a space that was her own. It would do for the moment. It was all fine.

Except that it wasn't. She missed Ian with every fiber of her being. Long nights were spent staring at the ceiling, wondering where he was, what he was thinking, what he was feeling. The truth was, it was never going to be fine without him. It was like she'd had hold

of the best thing in the world. For a week.
Until it slipped between her fingers.

Dutifully, Ian spent the next couple of weeks
going on dates with unmarried granddaughters of his grandfather's world. Hugo acceler-
ated the process to get Ian seen around town
with other women in order to diminish interest in the gossip photos with Laney. They
were women in the upper echelon, each and
every one from wealthy families who were
looking to make fortuitous matches that
would increase their already high standings
and statuses.

Abigail's lineage dated back to one of the
original founding families of Boston. She had
curly blond hair, an advanced degree and was
fluent in five languages. Ian couldn't find
words in any of the five to talk to her about.
She devoted most of her time to charities that
rescued kittens in need. Ian could tell from
the get-go that she wanted children and would
probably make a fine mother. It was also evi-
dent that she wanted to be in love above all
else, which Ian couldn't offer.

With Jordana, he tried—he really did—to
be interested in what type of granite coun-
tertops they'd want in the kitchen of the sub-

urban estate they'd build, as she thought the *only way* to raise children was out of the city. Although she showed him stone samples on her phone, on the small screen, he could barely discern the difference between Caledonia and Santa Cecilia, let alone choose one. Yes, his kind of marriage would be about planning and organization. But he couldn't bear the shrewdness of picking out kitchen materials on a first date.

Morgan was the beauty queen that obnoxious Connery spoke of in Bermuda. On a scale of one to ten, she was a definite eleven. Groomed and poised. In her tiny red dress, she wrapped her arm in his as she tottered on high heels into the restaurant. Where she inserted a bit of salad from her fork between her teeth so as to not muss her lipstick. While Ian certainly appreciated a woman with a pleasant appearance, Morgan's lacquered lips made him think of Laney.

It was Laney who he thought was beautiful. Her and only her. Beauty wasn't a stationary thing that someone's outer shell was adorned with. Beauty was an energy that radiated from Laney and onto him, and it was with her that he felt normal, complete. Beauty was a way of living.

After every woman his grandfather chose for him proved to be an intolerable match, he simply couldn't stand any more wife *shopping*.

He loved Laney.

What he felt for her was necessary, like oxygen. It was not something he could do without. He was going to marry, all right. Even if it meant falling out of favor with his family. He hoped it wouldn't come to that, but it was a measure of his love that he'd do anything to have her. He would start by talking to his grandfather.

"Grandson," Hugo said from his padded chair behind the enormous mahogany desk that had been his throne and office for as long as Ian could remember.

Ian sat in one of the leather chairs opposite him. He finished explaining that he had fallen in love with the woman in those leaked photos, a woman who had no pedigree, and he could let nothing stand in his way.

Hugo steepled his two index fingers on the desk. "You know I don't make arbitrary decisions, Ian. Everything I do, I do for a reason."

"Yes, and I have the utmost respect for you, what you've done for the company and, in turn, for our family. But I can't live without her. That is to say, I won't." He'd never spoken so demonstratively to his grandfather. Had never needed to.

"Then I'll have to be the wise one, as my own grandfather was."

Ian remembered the story of his great, great uncle being swindled by a dishonest woman. "And look at what happened to your uncle Harley, and that was with a baroness! Love cost Luss Global tens of millions of dollars in bad decisions because Harley was too distracted by matters of the heart to do his job."

"That's not the same situation, Grandfather. Harley and Nicole were wild. They drank brandy for breakfast. He never cared about Luss Global. She left him before they could have children, and now he's gallivanting around South America not doing a thing."

"That's all true. Which is why it's dangerous to make changes. When we don't deviate, our policies work, and have for generations. I'm trusting the future of the company to you, Ian. I need you to trust me back."

"I also need you to trust that I'm not one of my uncles. I will watch over and protect the company, just as you did. With Laney by my side, I'll be even stronger and lead Luss Global to even greater heights. I've seen how you and my father run your lives. You do it with singleness of purpose, and that has paid you back. But I'm different. I've always had a hunch that there was something else out there that I needed. Something that would not only inspire but would sustain me and allow me to reach my potential. And now that I've found it, I can't let it go. I'd be an empty shell without it."

His grandfather's face changed. He softened, making some of the deep wrinkles disappear. In an instant, he looked like a younger man. "I'd hoped to take this to my grave, Ian, but I'm going to tell you something."

So, his grandfather held a secret. And Ian had one of his grandmother's, one he'd never told a soul just as she'd asked.

"You think you're so different than I am? That I don't know what you're talking about? About emotion? About romance? I do."

Ian looked to him in question. "What do you mean?"

Hugo rubbed his chin. "I abided by the rules of my grandfather, your great-great-grandfather. My father chose my bride, your grandmother, the daughter of a financier from Philadelphia. We met only a couple of times before the wedding was arranged. Within a year, she gave birth to your father and then two years later to your uncle Harley. Two male heirs, plus managing the mansion we lived in with full-time staff, and my wife's work was done."

He paused for a moment and looked over to the photo of Rosalie he kept on his desk.

"You miss her, don't you?"

"Every day of my life." Hugo ran a finger back and forth along the top of the frame, almost like a caress. "As I was saying, within a couple of years, Rosalie's jobs as wife and mother were smoothly running operations, other than her worries about Harley always finding his way into mischief. I was ensconced here at the firm, to my father and grandfather's liking."

"Implementing your visions for what the company would become."

"One Sunday afternoon, after we'd been married for about six years, we were taking a walk in the formal garden. The sun was shining just so, creating what looked like copper flecks in your grandmother's hair. We were laughing about a comic drawing we'd seen in the newspaper. We laughed so hard and riotously, I took her hand and kissed the top of it. And…all at once… I realized that I was in love with her."

Ian's stomach jumped. He could hardly fathom what he was hearing! "You did?" That surely put a spin on his grandmother's secret.

"The conclusion almost knocked me off my feet. I suddenly saw my wife through the lens of someone who could never love anyone more, who could never obtain anything that made him feel as fulfilled as she did."

"Why didn't you tell her?" That was part of why his grandmother held her own secret, because she didn't know how Hugo felt.

"If she admitted to feeling the same, I was afraid I would get carried away spending time with her and not do my best for our company, just as my grandfather had feared. Or if she didn't love me that way in return, I would be heartbroken and unable to continue raising a family with her. It seemed the simplest and best decision to follow the Luss code of conduct, and conceal my true feelings. So, you see, I do know something about matters of the heart."

Ian balked at how difficult it must have been for his grandfather, if he felt like Ian did about Laney, to hold that truth inside of him. Especially not knowing the whole of it. Would his grandmother want Ian to act on her behalf and tell her husband what she'd buried all those years? Just so that he would know. And selfishly, might it help persuade him to let Ian and Laney pursue the future in open love? He silently asked his grandmother's spirit if he should reveal it now? Her answer was yes.

"She did."

"What?"

"Grandmother Rosalie did love you in return. Was in love with you."

Hugo's eyes became wet and milky, and a blush took over his usually pale cheeks. "How do you know?"

"Because she told me. Growing up, she was the only one who understood the person I was. She knew that going along with the family plan was going to be a hard path for me. So she told me because she thought it would help me not feel so apart from the rest of the family. That she was madly in love with you. But she didn't know if you were in love with her in return or if it would be acceptable to tell you how she felt, so she didn't. She also told me she'd meet you in heaven, although she didn't want you to rush to get there."

Hugo took an old-fashioned handkerchief out of his vest pocket and dabbed at his eyes.

He touched the framed photo again, staring at it as if the smile on her face had new meaning. Ian got up from his chair and went around to his grandfather's side of the desk, where they had a long, tight, love-filled hug.

"Ian, you've confirmed what her actions always said to me. Still, it's beautiful to hear it out loud. Your grandmother and I were fools to keep those words from each other. I don't want you to miss out on what we did." Hugo patted him briskly on the back. "You and your Laney go forth in love. I'll trust you."

CHAPTER TWELVE

EMANCIPATED BY THE conversation with his grandfather and the admissions that love had played more of a role in the Luss empire than was commonly thought, Ian was ready to reclaim his lifeblood. The agreement was made that Laney's humble beginnings shouldn't prohibit their union. Only he didn't know where to find her. A call to Clayton led to a call to Melissa. They were making plans for their belated honeymoon, which they'd changed to the Florida Keys.

Melissa was surprised that he was calling to find Laney. He hadn't told either of them about what happened in Bermuda and New York, and if he had to guess, Laney wouldn't have let on, either, especially given how things seemed to end with such finality.

Melissa answered, "She's working at a café in Dorchester. Do you want me to call her?"

"No. Can you text me the info? I'll just stop by." Dorchester. Where Shanice lived and Laney had grown up.

Arriving at the café, he went through its wooden front door with the scratched-up etched windows. Inside, the furniture was rickety, with tables and chairs anywhere they could fit. The old place needed some work, but he knew Laney liked character.

At the counter, a young woman with blue hair was ready to take his order. Looking left and right, he didn't see Laney, so he asked if she was there.

"She's off today."

Disappointment deflated him. He should have called first. "Is she in tomorrow?"

"Yeah, at eleven. Do you want anything?"

Yes, he thought. He'd rather sit at a table for a while and try to feel Laney's presence than go home to his big empty bachelor pad. "Cappuccino, please."

He took a small table and sat with his back to the wall so he could people-watch the entire space. He surveyed the staff. They looked like a friendly bunch who worked well together. A very thin man whose arms were covered with tattoos looked like he might be the one in charge.

After Ian sipped his drink for a few minutes, the tattooed man passed by and asked him, "How's it going?"

"Is this your café?"

"No, I'm the manager, Theo. Is there a problem?"

"No, not at all. I was just curious who owns it."

"That's Mr. and Mrs. Giordano. But now the place is up for sale. They're retiring."

Ian's ears perked up. "Really. Would you happen to know which real estate agent is handling the listing?"

"I can find out for you. Give me a minute."

The smile that crossed Ian's lips had enough wattage to light up the city.

"Someone was in looking for you yesterday," blue-haired Cora blurted as soon as Laney came around the counter to put her bag away.

That was strange. Who would be looking for her? No one even knew that she worked here. It had only been a few days. "Who was it?"

"It was a he. He didn't leave his name, but if you have no use for him, you send him my way, okay?"

Laney chuckled. So an attractive man was looking for her. As mysterious as that sounded, she couldn't imagine who it was. Maybe it was a mistake. Or maybe it was a customer. It wasn't Enrique; he was back in Spain.

There's no way it was… No, she stopped that thought before it could go any further. Impossible. She shrugged her shoulders.

Her first task of the day was to inventory the paper goods and see what needed to be ordered. As she did, her eyes wandered around. This would be a nice enough place to work. For a while. She needed to make the best of it. In addition to the failure of the café in Pittsfield and the disaster that was Enrique, now she had yet another piece of emotional baggage to learn how to carry around. Ian. For the rest of her life, it would be Ian. Her one true love.

What was he doing right now, she wondered as she completed her task? Probably having a grand date with a refined woman from a prestigious family. Maybe he was taking her on a horse-drawn carriage ride in New York's Central Park.

No! That was only for her. She couldn't bear the idea of him doing that with someone else. That was hers. She swiped a couple of tears away with the backs of her fingers, then quickly washed her hands at the sink. There was no crying at work. No matter how much she missed the man she loved.

"Laney."

She heard a voice behind her so familiar she was sure she was hallucinating. Wow, the mind was strong. Had she just been thinking so hard about him that now she was hearing his voice? What was next, having a memory of his arms around her? And as soon as she thought that, she did have the sense that his long and strong limbs were encircling her, pulling them into the private world that was each other's salvation.

"Laney."

She turned around. It hadn't been her imagination. Ian was standing right there, just like when they surprised each other by being on the plane to Bermuda. Here, the metal counter was the only thing separating them. Words came out of her mouth that didn't even sound like hers.

"What are you doing here?"

"What do you think? I came to find you."

"Why?"

"Because I love you."

Laney's heart thumped in her chest. Both of them knew they had fallen in love at Pink

Shores but had never said the taboo words to each other. Now he was here saying them.

"And we're going to be together for the rest of our lives."

"I thought that wasn't possible."

"It's the only thing that's possible."

"What about your family?"

"It's time for a reevaluation. My grandfather and I are working it out."

"What do you mean?"

"I'll tell you all about it later. Meanwhile, I have a present for you."

He came bearing gifts. Laney was overwhelmed. This was so abrupt and so unlikely. Yet she wasn't going to deny that she wanted to be with him just as much as he was claiming to want to be with her. Could it be real? That love was in her cards of fortune, after all.

"What's the gift?"

Ian swept his arm from left to right across the café. "This."

"What?"

"The café."

"What about it?"

"I bought it for you."

"You what?" Now she really thought she was hallucinating. "How did you even know it was for sale?"

"Theo told me." He pointed to the manager, who gave them a thumbs-up signal. "I was here yesterday."

"Okay."

"Okay?" Ian read the displeased expression on her face. "What's wrong?"

"I want to own my own café!" she exclaimed. "I mean, it's beyond beautiful of you to offer, but I don't want to be in business with someone again. This is something I want to do for myself."

Ian's eyes became drawn and his face drooped into sadness.

Oh. She hadn't meant to shut him down like that, but he shouldn't have taken such a drastic action without talking to her about it first. She didn't want to be responsible to someone else if she failed, couldn't go through that again.

She watched inside his eyes as something bubbled. He swiped open his phone and did some furious tapping. Coming up for air, he announced, "Okay, Laney Sullivan. You are now the owner. You will make payments of—" he said and showed her a number on his phone's screen "—every month for five years, at which point you will own it outright. Do we have a deal?"

Laney's breath became fast and heavy. This was terrifying. "Ian, I…"

"There are two conditions of the sale."

Oh, here it comes. Everything always had a hitch. "What are those?"

"The first one is that you come around from that counter."

She slipped by Cora, who didn't even try to seem like she wasn't watching all of this take place. Same with Theo and a couple of other staff members.

"What's the other condition?"

"That no matter what happens with the café or Luss Global or any other business we might be in, that you'll be mine forever."

She threw her arms around his neck, and he wrapped his around her waist and spun her until her feet left the ground.

"You drive a hard bargain, Ian Luss. I accept."

She gave him a kiss to seal the deal.

* * * * *

If you enjoyed this story, check out these other great reads from Andrea Bolter

Adventure with a Secret Prince
Caribbean Nights with the Tycoon
Wedding Date with the Billionaire
Captivated by Her Parisian Billionaire

All available now!